LINDSEY N. RHODEN

A LOVE WOVEN IN MOONLIGHT

A NOVELLA

To my very own Bastian.

Thank you for continuously helping me heal.

CONTENT WARNING

This novella discusses themes of infertility, intense grief and loss, assault/abuse on page, and a scene of intense violence on page. Content warnings should be taken seriously and read before diving into the story. Please make sure you feel comfortable with these trigger warnings before continuing. Your mental health matters.

Playlist

- ▶ **HOLD ON**
  ALEXIA EVELLYN

- ▶ **MY HOME**
  MYLES SMITH

- ▶ **WHAT WAS I MADE FOR?**
  BILLIE EILISH

- ▶ **LITTLE RUNAWAY**
  BENSON BOONE

- ▶ **RIVER**
  MYLSE SMITH

- ▶ **SOMETHING IN THE ORANGE**
  ZACH BRYAN

- ▶ **I FOUND**
  AMBER RUN

- ▶ **RUNNING WITH THE WOLVES**
  AURORA

- ▶ **ALL THAT REALLY MATTERS**
  ILLENIUM, TEDDY SWIMS

CHAPTER I
AERIE

The breeze was calm and welcoming as my sisters and I walked through the woods. The moon hung low tonight, its fullness unmistakable as it beckoned us out into the wilderness. These nights were some of my favorites, walking hand in hand with the females I now considered my family. They were the sole reason I ever came to understand the meaning of the word. It didn't mean anything to me before—it was just a word used to manipulate those in your bloodline.

But with them? With them it was different. They were love and joy, tenderness and kindness. They were warm cups of tea in the midafternoon sun and long walks at night under the full moon. They were my sisters—my home.

Before long, we slowed as we entered a small clearing. Its familiarity was a welcome feeling as we set up the fire and spread out the soft cotton blankets we'd brought with us. Flora wasted no time laying out the dishes of food and containers of full moon tea she'd prepared just for tonight. I inhaled deeply as the sweet smell of vanilla filled the air. Flora's tea cakes were a delicacy we didn't often get to experience. But on full moon nights, she was always armed with some sort of delicious rarity for us to enjoy.

We ate and drank till our hearts were content under the light of the moon, soaking in the steadying vibrations and cleansing energy of the silver rays against our skin. Serafina strummed the strings of her lyre, humming along to the sweet melody as Flora and Luna held hands, dancing around the fire and through the clearing. Some might call it witchcraft, a ritual of sorts. In a lot of ways, I suppose it was. It had felt weird to me when I first joined them—to let myself go and just experience nature on a wholly new level.

We came out here to pay tribute, worshiping the world around us and accepting the gifts it bestowed on us. Whether it be healing, peace, power… the moon listened and received our needs. And for those who were patient enough to still their spirits and listen, she'd speak back. There was magic there, a kind I'd never been able to experience before, when I slowed down enough to truly listen and look within nature itself. When I took the time to see and feel and accept the world around me in a different way—a purer way.

It was woven in the grass beneath my feet and the moonlight upon my skin—something strong and freeing. It took me several moons to get used to the feeling and truly participate in these nights. But once I did, I finally understood.

This was living.

I threw my head back, letting my long white tresses fall down my back and sway in the wind. Flame licked at the wood piled in the middle of the clearing, growing higher as a chorus of crackles filled the trees around us. The night's air had a crisp chill to it, and I was glad for the warmth from the fire as it crept over my exposed skin. My bare toes scrunched in the damp grass and soil beneath them, grounding me to the earth itself just as the moon connected me to the cosmos above.

I was here. I was alive. I was safe.

If I had told myself any of those statements a decade ago, I would have thought myself delusional. My father's estate was not safe for me. I may have been alive, but it wasn't living. Most days I felt as if I was in a fog, not fully here or there. Our bloodline had been in hiding for centuries, veiled from the New Magic who sought our demise. I couldn't blame them, not after everything the fae had done to the mortals and those with *lesser* magic. The fae were a vicious breed, and it was only fitting for the Fates to tear down the pedestals they'd built for themselves.

That was the life I was born into—one of captivity. And it was my own blood who held me captive. It didn't matter that I wasn't like them, that I couldn't fathom the amount of hatred it would take to treat another—*any other*—being the way I'd heard about in their tales of glory. Though my father's bragging could not always be trusted, he was still certainly one of the cruelest fae. When he spoke of New Magic, seething rage ran hot through him. I knew firsthand because I was usually on the receiving end of that rage.

I shook out the memories, my eyes catching on Esme over the flames of the fire, across the clearing. She watched me with careful intent, her ebony hair rippling behind her gracefully in the soft breeze. A smile slipped over her lips as she waited for me to begin, nodding at me in encouragement. I stretched out my hands and welcomed the moonlight to wash over me, to replace those thoughts and fears with the energy it offered up tonight.

Esme mimicked my movements, dancing opposite me across the fire. I lost track of her before long, seeing only a blur of fiery orange and the flash of hands and hair trailing around the clearing as the four of us lost ourselves to the music Serafina strummed. I threw myself around the fire, pouring all of my energy into my movements—every horrible memory, every haunting secret, and asking for the moon to cleanse me of it all. I don't know how long I danced, how long Serafina played, but I collapsed on the forest floor, chest heaving and head turned upward as the moonlight washed over me. I stayed there for several moments, basking in the feeling of the rays still dancing along my skin—so long that I hadn't even realized when the music had stopped.

"Aerie," Luna called to me, patting a spot beside her on a blanket next to the blazing fire. A smile spread across my face, eyes opening to the sight of my sisters circling around the fire. I rose quickly, bounding over to her on feet light as air as I left my worries behind and dove into the promise of what tonight offered: a chance for restoration, healing, and connection with my sisters and the nature around us.

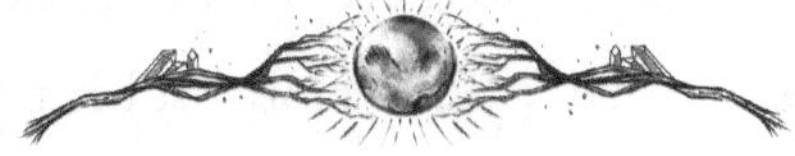

The midday sun broke through the trees, its buttery rays falling softly on my face and rousing me from my sleep. I rubbed lazily at my eyes, acclimating them to the brightness of the day before opening them fully. My body tingled with the power still ebbing through me. The moon had been gracious last night, a resounding sense of peace and strength echoing through me. The ritual had fortified my magic, but more than anything, it had calmed my mind.

Turning over, I saw Esme's rich umber eyes as she hummed in pleasure of the restful night's sleep. "I'll never get used to feeling the energy after a full moon ritual," she purred, stretching her arms out wide as she sat up. She ran her hands through her thick black hair, grimacing as she plucked a bit of moss from the silky strands. "Even if it means spending a night on the forest floor instead of my warm bed."

I covered my mouth, trying to hide the giggle that escaped my lips.

"If you two are done with your beauty sleep, we could use your help packing up," Flora called out from the other side of the firepit that had long since stopped burning. Only the faintest remnants of smoke swirled into the morning air.

Esme gave me an exaggerated eye roll as she called back across the clearing, "Yes, mother." Both Flora and her sister Luna had taken on the roles of caretakers for our little coven. As much as we appreciated their caring nature, we also never missed a moment to tease them for it. We both tried to suppress our laughs as Flora cut us a look that could kill, knocking us both on our asses with a flick of her wrist as the blanket beneath us jerked away and landed softly in her hands.

"Show-off," I mumbled under my breath, only loud enough for Esme to hear, as we scrambled to our feet and wiped the dirt and leaves from our skirts.

CHAPTER 2
AERIE

The kitchen of our little cottage was bustling with activity. We worked in harmonized synchronicity as we prepared supper. We'd spent the day resting after our long trek home and cleaning up after the full moon ritual, rejoining each other for supper preparations once the sun began sinking lower in the sky. Luna took up a spot by the stove, stirring and tasting whatever concoction she'd thrown together for us. The scent of fresh rosemary and stewed meat filled the cottage. My mouth watered as I waited for her to finish. You could never tell what exactly she was making until it was done, but it somehow always turned out perfect. I'd never tasted food better than hers.

I prepared to brew a round of tea for the afternoon beside Luna, pulling a mixture of herbs and tea leaves from the hutch. I'd already set out a round of teacups on the counter, their delicate floral prints faded from years of use. Flora was busying herself with tidying up the small kitchen, but stopped here and there to peek over my shoulder and check on me. When I stepped away to put the kettle on the stove, she snuck a few more ingredients into the mortar and threw me a wink.

I shook my head at her as I felt the smile creep over my face, knowing the herbs she'd selected happened to be her favorite. I wouldn't argue, though. She'd taught me everything I knew about herbs.

It had been almost two years since I'd joined the coven, but I was still the most recent addition—the baby of the family. From what they'd shared with me, the coven started with Flora and Luna, sisters who had once belonged to Talamh, the earth tribe. Their parents had been farmers on the outskirts of the tribe's borders, choosing to live a life away from society due to their interest in witchcraft. They were kind, loving parents, based on the way Luna and Flora lit up whenever they talked about them. This had been their childhood home—one built by the light and love carefully cultivated by their parents. There were still carvings etched on the wall from where their parents marked their heights as they grew throughout the years. It might have been a simple home, but it was one filled with warm memories.

That is, until some of the tribe's members decided they weren't comfortable with members who practiced witchcraft. Back in the early days after New Magic took over, people were confused and scared of anything that felt too similar to Old Magic. The tribe's members came to them on a new moon night and demanded their lives. Though they spared the young Flora and Luna, they were still forced to watch their parents dragged out and burned alive. The sisters didn't talk about that dark day often. But every now and then, when the night grew still and their spirits restless, they shared small glimpses of the torment that still haunted them—some primal need to speak with their new family about the ones who raised them taking over. It was on nights like these that they were forced to admit they would never be able to leave this place, dedicated to carry on the humble, untamed life their parents had built here.

I knew their pain, the pain of being rejected by the world of New Magic. After leaving my father's estate, I'd tried to find a place amongst the Tribes. As a fae, I was only met with hatred and fear. That eventually drove me to the outskirts of the Tribes' borders—drove me here, to this makeshift family that took me in with open arms and only a few questions asked.

Flora and Luna had already taken in two more before me, Esme and Serafina. They'd explained to me the purpose of their coven, to provide a home for those who had nowhere else to go. And as I was caught in the tide of their love, I began to understand the passion behind their purpose.

The whistle of the kettle pulled me from my thoughts. I dusted the remnants of dried herbs from my hands as I pivoted towards the stove and grabbed the kettle with a towel.

"Tea almost ready?" Esme asked, emerging from her bedroom and crossing gracefully through the sitting room and into the kitchen. She came up beside me, yawning from the nap she'd insisted on taking in her own bed after our night under the full moon. I rolled my eyes, stifling a small laugh as she caught me, landing a small nudge against my hip in jest.

Esme might tease often, a quick wit and a hearty laugh never far from her lips, but she had a sort of refined grace about her that she almost couldn't help. Even with my fae upbringing, I'd never enjoyed learning how to be polished. I was a rebellious child, a free spirit who fought with every ounce of my being. Esme, it seemed, was made for the highborn life. Elegance flowed through her like the blood in her veins, and she would have made a fantastic highborn for Scaldor—the Fire Tribe—some day. That is, if her family hadn't stripped her of her titles and disinherited her. All because they didn't agree with the lifestyle she'd chosen for herself, didn't agree with who she truly believed herself to be. They couldn't fathom accepting her as a leader without her claiming her *rightful* place—tethered to a male bloodline. Seeing her here now, standing amongst my sisters and every bit the definition of grace and elegance, I couldn't understand how her family could ever reject her like they had. But her story was mine too, in many ways. Hurt by family who refused to understand us. Rejected by blood for wanting a different life for ourselves.

Her umber eyes sparkled as she watched me pour the steaming water over the crushed leaves in each individual teacup. I couldn't help but smile, eagerness radiating off her. I set the kettle down and handed her a steaming cup. She took it and brought the warm liquid to her nose, inhaling deeply at the rich, earthy scent. I grabbed my own cup and turned around, leaning back against the counter and looking through the archway into the cozy sitting room beside the kitchen. The first floor of our cottage was an open space, the rooms separated only by old wooden beams, most often occupied by whatever harvest we were drying from the gardens just outside the kitchen. Esme turned to mirror me as we breathed in the familiar comfort of our home—the space riddled with overflowing shelves of well loved books, woven rugs, and ancient, rugged furniture.

My eyes finally landed on Serafina, her small form curled up in the corner of the sitting room on the window seat. Her blonde curls fell over her face, her nose buried in a book and a knit blanket pulled securely around her shoulders. Our nights under the full moon usually refreshed our energy, even Serafina was often more emboldened than normal after. But judging how she shied away from the supper preparations, I couldn't help but feel the weight of whatever spirits still tormented her soul.

I tilted my head toward Esme, noticing her attention landing in the same spot as mine. "Is she doing okay?" I asked, tipping my chin in her direction.

Esme watched her for a moment longer before turning back to the counter and grabbing another cup of tea. "Give us a minute," was her only explanation as she strode delicately through the kitchen and into the sitting room. I watched them for a moment longer, a small grin spreading across my lips as I noted the endearing way Esme looked after her.

Serafina had always been reserved. She'd found the coven before me, but was still so quiet about her past, about what troubles led her to this way of life. I related to her in that way—so hesitant to let the details of my past be fully known to the others, so scared about them discovering the darkness of all my secrets. I'd let bits out here and there, but even after all our time together the idea of letting them see all of me was too daunting to face.

Still, Serafina seemed to struggle more than me. She was so shy, so closed off in almost every way. And I couldn't help but wonder what atrocities she'd experienced to make her so hesitant. Esme seemed to be the only one who could pull her out of that isolation. As I watched the way Esme nestled herself beside her, letting her fingers trail softly over Serafina's ivory skin, I wondered if it could possibly be something beyond friendship I saw growing between them. Suddenly feeling like I was intruding, I turned my attention back to the kitchen.

Luna was finishing up the stew, Flora beside her at the stove preparing bowls. I placed my cup in my usual spot on the kitchen table before setting the sisters cups in their respective spots and helping them set the rest of the table for supper.

"Esme, Serafina," I called over my shoulder, grimacing at the thought of disturbing them. "Supper's ready."

Flora moved around the table in fluid grace as she set the bowls down, Luna following in her footsteps with fresh baked bread. I took my seat, noticing the vibrant yellow of the sunflowers Serafina had foraged on our walk back to the cottage this morning.

Within minutes, the entire coven was seated around the table, breaking bread and waiting to dive in bowls of warm, aromatic stew. The center of the table was full of an assortment of fruits and cheeses arranged around Seraphina's flowers, small glittering chunks of crystals accenting the spread in a delightful display of purples and silvers. Despite my father's court having been practically nonexistent once he went into hiding, I grew up with one of the best cooks in all the fae realms and ate at some of the most elegantly dressed tables. But as I looked down upon the table full of food made with such love and care, I didn't think I'd ever seen anything more delicious in my life.

Esme leaned in to Serafina seated beside her and whispered something that brought the hint of a smile to Serafina's lips. I hid my own behind my hands as I unfolded the tawny linen napkin Flora had set out on each place setting. Luna cleared her throat from the end of the table. In answer, our heads turned to Flora seated at the opposite end, as we waited for her to bless the supper.

"May the sun shine brightly upon us today," Flora began our prayer. "May the moon take tender care of us through the night. May the earth bless us with its provisions and may the air fill our lungs with love and light. Blessed be."

We echoed her prayer before diving into the spread of food. Nothing but the sound of clinking dishes filled the intimate space as we passed the trays of bread and cheese around and ate heartily. We flowed so well amidst each other, finding a steady rhythm as if we'd spent our lives within the movement of one another. Any outsider would think we were truly sisters, but Flora and Luna were the only ones related by blood, much wiser and seasoned in life and witchcraft. Esme and I acted like mirror reflections of one another, teasing Flora any chance we could get and looking after Serafina as if she were the younger sister that needed our guidance and protection. We fluctuated between sisters and children, friends and mentors, as often as the moon rose and fell.

Eventually our bellies filled and conversation started flowing. I looked around the table, suddenly overcome with the amount of love and acceptance I'd found here. My life before this was one of heartache and misery—one I often thought about ending just out of desperation to escape. But now, suddenly, I realized where my life's thread must have been leading me. I was thankful for my need to persevere, my need to find what else was out there besides fae wrath and captivity. It was not all for nothing. It was leading me here to this moment all that time, to my sisters, my family that had taken me in and shown me what it looked like to rely on others—to *love* others.

It was leading me home.

CHAPTER 3
AERIE

After supper, I slipped upstairs to ready myself for bed, digging around in my small wardrobe and pulling out a simple cotton nightdress. Despite the night beneath the moon, I couldn't shake the thoughts that had begun to haunt me tonight. I opened the window, letting the moonlight pour in as I tried to recenter myself. But my mind still drifted between worlds, thinking of my life before I'd found the coven.

I rolled my shoulders, trying to loosen the thoughts from my mind as I shrugged off my clothes from the day and let the nightdress slip over my body, brushing against my ankles. I couldn't help but notice the many knots that sleeping beneath the stars had left in my hair, and I grabbed my brush and a book before heading back downstairs.

The sound of the crackling fire filled our cozy sitting room as each of us found a place to settle into. I scooped the patchwork quilt off the back of the sofa and wrapped it around my shoulders as I moved to take my seat. Tucking my legs beneath me, I sunk into the well loved sofa and cherished the warmth of the fire prickling my skin. Our teacups from dinner lay scattered throughout the room, landing on any available surface—the precarious edge of an armchair, on the woven rug beside Esme's feet, balanced carefully in the crevice of Luna's arm as she read. Flora floated around us and refilled them. I hummed in appreciation as she handed me mine, taking a deep sip, feeling grounded by the notes of honeyed chamomile.

Serafina was opposite me, curled up again with the book she'd been reading earlier. Esme was close by, hovering over her but far enough away to respect her space, pretending to be distracted with the embroidery in her hands. The two exchanged stolen glances with each other, quickly returning to the tasks in hand in an effort to not be noticed. I dipped my head to hide my growing smile. Luna nudged my foot with hers from the sofa beside me, the creases of her face deepening as she flashed a tight smile my way. Flora set the teapot on a small table in the middle of the room and took her place beside Luna, opening her notebook and no doubt adding an account of the previous night's festivities.

We didn't spend every night like this. Some nights we broke off to our rooms or fluttered around the cottage, working on our own various tasks, lost to our own worlds. But others, we sat down together in this room, bathing in the firelight and enjoying the simple presence of each other as we read or stitched or simply just watched the flames dance in the hearth.

Joy filled my heart, thinking about how many of those nights I'd enjoyed in this room with them. But a tinge of grief echoed somewhere deep, drawing my thoughts back to how many nights in comparison I'd spent alone and scared within my father's court. I fiddled with the brush in my hands, working at the tangles in the ends of my hair as my thoughts drifted to those horrifying nights.

"Here, let me," Luna offered, reaching over the edge of our sofas as she gently placed her hand on mine and took the brush. When I looked to her, she offered me a warm smile. I couldn't help but wonder if she knew my mind was elsewhere tonight.

"Alright," I answered softly as I turned toward the fire and let my hair cascade down my back for her to work on. The motion of her tenderly working the brush through my hair was soothing to my soul. I closed my eyes, completely spellbound by her gesture, imagining what it could have been like to grow up with a mother or an older sister to take care of me in my youth.

"It's okay, you know." Luna's words broke me from my thoughts, pulling my attention back to her.

"What's okay?" I asked as I stared ahead into the depths of the flames before me, already knowing her answer.

"To ask for help." She paused, her hands stilling against my hair. "To let us in."

The color drained from my face, my stomach suddenly turning at the thought of sharing with them all the darkness that my past held. I looked over to Serafina, incapable of missing the way her own color had depleted, her eyes focused too forcefully on the pages before her. Neither of us had shared much about our pasts, about whatever spirits still haunted us. I knew Luna was saying this for more than just my benefit.

I looked over my shoulder at Luna. Her kind eyes, wise with years of experience, gleamed with the hope and love that only a sister could have. Flora leaned into her, wrapping her arms around Luna as she too watched me.

"What is family for," added Flora, "if not to lean on when our burdens get too heavy to carry on our own?"

Tears stung behind my eyes as I swallowed hard to keep them from spilling. I could feel the weight of those burdens in the faint scars covering my back beneath the blanket and nightdress I clung to—could feel its weight in the fear that rooted inside me every time one of my sisters tried not to look at the ones I couldn't hide. I hesitated, nodding slightly as I turned my head back to the rest of the room. Esme glanced at me, a small, tender smile playing at her lips.

"That goes for you too, Serafina," Flora called out across the room. Serafina glanced up from her novel to throw a tentative smile Flora's way, but quickly dove back into the book, hiding behind the pages. I understood the sentiment, pulling my blanket tighter around me as I brought my knees up to my chest and turned back to the fire.

"We may not understand everything you have been through," Luna pressed on. "But we have been through our own fair share of heartache and grief. And more than anything, we want you girls to feel like this is your home too, your safe haven."

"I do," I answered quickly. I spun towards her, facing her fully now. "You all have done so much to make me feel welcome and accepted." I took Luna's hands in my own. "I cannot say enough about how much I appreciate your kindness, your love. You *are* my family. I could never think otherwise."

"Agreed." The sound of Serafina's voice shocked me, pulling my tearful gaze from Luna's matching one. Serafina peeked over her book, a sort of fierce sincerity shining from her as she found the courage to speak up.

"Good," Luna finally answered after several moments of powerful silence had passed. She patted my hand, finally letting go of my grasp as she turned back to her sister. "Flora and I may be blood, but we are all sisters here. We just need to check in every now and then and be sure you remember that too."

Flora patted her sister reassuringly on the arm, before pulling a basket into her lap from the floor beside her. "And as my sisters, I'm sure you all would love to lend me a helping hand tonight!"

My groan echoed across the room as I caught sight of Esme rolling her eyes.

"Oh, hush now," chided Flora. "How will I ever be able to pass along my wisdom if you lot refuse to partake in lessons and practice? I've had to stoop as low as guilting you into helping me out of sheer familial obligation." She handed groupings of plants to each of us. My fingers already burned from the next hour of bundling that I knew was in store for us.

"Now remember how I taught you." Flora moved about the sitting room as she lectured, watching us carefully as we began our work. "Tight, even weaves. Make sure you are grouping the leaves together in the proper sizes and whatever you do, don't mix herbs."

Flora was always one for a teachable moment, striving to pour as much education into each of us as we would allow her to. Bundling and drying the herbs was an important chore for all of our spellwork, and it was one I knew none of us truly minded helping with. Even so, we loved to tease Flora too much to let her know that. Esme attempted to hide her smile, something like amusement shining from Serafina's usually guarded eyes. Luna sent a lighthearted elbow into my side when I failed to stifle a laugh at Flora's instructions, like we hadn't already done this a million times before.

"Sister," Luna cut in gingerly. "Perhaps you could read to us. To pass the time as we work?" Flora eyed her, considering for a moment.

"Oh, alright," she relented, finally giving in. "But only if you promise to double check your work." She pointed a finger at each of us before striding over to a nearby bookshelf and looking over the collection.

"Yes, mother," Esme and I said in unison. It snipped the last tether of composure we had as the others burst into laughter. It was Flora's turn to roll her eyes, making her way back with her book selection and settling into a rocking chair by the fire.

"You laugh now, but you won't find it so funny when you accidentally poison a person you're trying to heal because you didn't verify your herbal identification before performing your spellwork," she scolded. But even Flora wasn't immune to the contagious laughter that now filled the sitting room.

"Alright, alright. Hush now or I won't be able to get through a single page of this story." Her joyous tone was warm and loving as her words reached out through the room. I took a deep breath, relishing this time together as she started reading from the battered, leatherbound book cradled carefully in her hands. Her words, mixed with the gently crackling fire and the slow creak of her chair, quickly became the only sound among us as we sat in euphoric silence. I fell into a spellbound sense of calm as I bundled the herbs, enchanted by the myth she'd decided to read to us. It was a story full of deception and scheming, some ancient tale about the gods and the Fates and the history of this world from a time before even I knew.

She could have chosen any book from that shelf and I would have sat here all the same—eager to listen, eager to learn. It wasn't the content that mattered, but the love with which she poured it into us. It was that love that made me want to find the courage to open up to them. Each of my sisters held such a special place in my heart. I knew Luna was right, that someday I would have to let them in. In the depths of my soul, I knew it would only help me. But letting go of that secret was too heavy a weight to bear. It was easier for now to carry it alone, to keep them free from that nightmare—even if it was just for a moment longer. The time would come, one day, when I'd no longer be able to endure on my own. When I'd feel ready to finally let go.

Perhaps that would be the day that I could finally, truly move on from *his* grasp. For now, it sat tucked away in some dark recess of my mind.

Even now I shuffled to pull the quilt up higher as I worked at the bundle of rosemary in my hands, ensuring it didn't slip far enough down to reveal the marks that marred my skin. I knew that day was coming sooner rather than later. I owed it to them to be honest. But I didn't know how to balance my obligation to them with my own fear of letting go of that part of myself. Even two years later, this all felt so new to me, having a family I could trust and rely on. I looked around the room at my sisters, working together to take care of one another. And I couldn't help but let that hope ignite—that some day I'd find the courage to truly let them see all of me.

CHAPTER 4
AERIE

*T*he tile of my childhood home was cool beneath my bare feet. The hallway was dark, vacant, as some younger version of myself tiptoed towards my father's chambers. I screamed at her to stop, to turn back. She wouldn't like what she found there, wouldn't be able to escape his cruelty if she pushed onward. I stopped short, noticing the crack of light escaping the partially closed door ahead.

I took a deep breath, holding it as I crept forward. I peered through the small slit, my heart dropping with fear when I couldn't catch sight of my father. Back then, I wasn't sure what curiosity pulled me from bed and pushed me to wander towards his chambers. Back then I didn't know what I was looking for. Now though—now I knew I was just a desperate, love deprived, scared little girl hoping to find some sort of comfort.

I stifled a scream as the door burst open, my father's eyes blazing like a fire. He stared down at me, rage emanating in his magic *wrapped arms. After a moment, his face softened as his hand caressed my cheek.*

"My little Aermidh," he hummed in slurred words. Before I knew what was happening, he grabbed my arm and dragged me into the room, close to the light of the fire burning in the hearth. He stared at me for a long time, hands gripping my arms so hard it hurt. I felt the hot tears begin to stream down my face—too scared to make a noise due to the crazed sort of intrigue burning in his eyes

"You, my child," he finally said. "You will be our saving grace, the light for our people." He turned towards the firelight, a wicked glint igniting in his gaze. He reached out a hand, harnessing a flame within his grasp. "Even if the rest of the world must burn at your hand."

Within an instant he thrust the flame into my hands, the hands of a child not yet come into their powers—hands that would burn trying to harness magic beyond her years. My screams tore through the room, bouncing off the walls and echoing down the halls of the empty estate. It didn't matter how loud I screamed—how raw my throat felt or how much I ran. There was no one here who would save me, no one coming to free me from the fae king's insanity. He'd hidden us away from the rest of the world. Not to keep me safe, but because I was nothing more than a secret weapon for him to reclaim his "rightful" place. I observed the little girl trying with all her might to win her father's favor, no matter the pain that he would inflict—and I pitied her. She was so young, so desperate for his love. I knew now that he'd do anything to force me to do his bidding, to bring the fae back into power. Even if the rest of the world burned at my hand—and I with it.

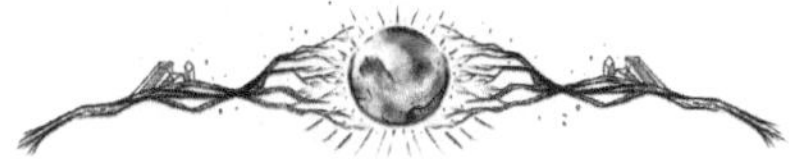

I awoke with a start, bolting upright in my bed. My breath was ragged, as if I'd been holding it while dreaming, and a cold sweat had broken out over my skin. I looked down at my shaking hands, letting my fingers unfurl and release the tension I'd been holding in my clenched fists. By the moonlight streaming through a nearby window, I could make out the faintest remnants of the scars on my palms. The fae were known for their fast healing, but there was only so much my fae blood could do when the wounds had been reopened night after night, decade after decade.

Even now, after being free of him for so long, the scars were still there. Faint, yes, but not gone completely. I absent-mindedly ran my hands over the other parts of my body covered in similar marks. Father had always been one for lessons. And he'd been sure to start them young, far before a fae child should have been dealing with such things. Feeling the marks now, every rough patch of skin helped remind me that I'd escaped. I'd gotten away. And I'd never again have to feel pain at his hand, nor endure his rage and insanity.

A soft knock on the door pulled me from my thoughts. I looked up to find Luna lingering by the entrance to my room, watching me with a careful, loving gaze.

"I heard you dreaming. Thought I'd come check on you." She offered a kind smile as she waited for permission to enter.

"You weren't sleeping?" I asked as I gestured her into the room. She made her way towards the bed, stopping by the window to look out at the moon.

"Oh, you know me. Always been more of a night owl. The moon's awake, so I'm awake."

I huffed out a laugh as she perched on the edge of my bed, perfectly cast in the stream of moonlight. She was the perfect opposite of her sister. Where Flora was sunshine, green grass, and bubbly springs with beautiful waterfalls, Luna was a peaceful starry night full of watchful owls and a soft breeze. I looked up to them both in so many ways—they were strength and love, filling the gaps for each other. And now Luna was here, watching me like she knew every torment ravaging my body without me even saying them out loud.

"Do you want to talk about it?" Her words were soft, genuine. She wouldn't press me if I still wasn't willing to share. She just wanted me to know she was here if I needed her to be. I nodded slowly, blinking away the tears in my eyes. Luna nodded sympathetically, her eyes widening as she realized I'd finally agreed to talk. She stood quickly, patting me on the leg. "Let me go make some tea first."

With that, she was out the door and down the stairs. I forced my still shaking body out of bed and rummaged through my wardrobe, finding a thick, wool blanket and draping it over my shoulders to guard against the crisp night air. I took a steadying breath to calm my nerves before heading downstairs to join her.

Luna was already setting cups up on the veranda outside. A fire burned in the hearth, a kettle hanging above it as the sweet scent of chamomile and lavender trailed through the sitting room. I breathed in the scent, welcoming its already calming properties. I grabbed the kettle off the fire with a towel and poured its contents into the teapot Luna had set out for us. Clutching my blanket in one hand to keep it pulled tight around me, and the teapot with the towel in the other, I made my way out on the veranda to join her.

The night was quiet, only the slight chirping of crickets and the occasional windswept rustling of leaves accompanying us as we settled into our chairs. I sank back, pulling my cup of tea tight into my chest. I inhaled the steam as it rose to meet me while Luna stirred a spoonful of honey into her cup, her jade ring catching in the firelight with the motion. We sat in the silence of the moment, letting the restful music of the night wash over us, grounding us as we sat back and listened, sipping from our cups.

"Was it one of your nightmares again?" Luna finally asked. I nodded, unsure how else to answer.

"Your father?" Luna questioned

I set my cup down on the wrought-iron table between us.

"Yes, it seems that it's always him when nightmares come to me." I stole a glance at my now empty hands.

"He's the one that gave you those, isn't he?" Luna must have seen where my gaze fell. I grasped at the edges of my blanket, resituating it across my shoulders as an excuse to bury the scars she was asking about, nodding timidly as I did so.

"I thought so." She paused, taking a sip from her cup before continuing: "You've always known that it's not a requirement to share here. But I meant what I said earlier. It's okay to let us in, let us help if we can. You haven't told us much about your past. Just that you were trying to escape your father's wrath and needed a place to hide. If there's something we can do to help, we want to. But we can't do that unless you tell us what happened."

Shame bloomed in my chest. I hadn't told them much about my past because I was frightened they wouldn't accept me if they knew every dark thing that my father had made me do. But perhaps it was time to let them in, let *someone* see every side of who I was, even the sides I was most ashamed of. Maybe this is what the full moon ritual had given me. I'd asked for peace, healing. Maybe this was the journey to it.

"My father..." I started, pausing to collect my thoughts. "He was insane, out of his mind after the Fates took down the fae kingdoms. He couldn't cope without that power; it drove him mad to lose everything like that. And living in hiding for all those years only pushed him further into that madness."

I reached out to take another sip of my tea, jumping slightly as Luna reached out a hand to stop me.

"You don't have to defend him, Aerie. Whatever he did to you... There is no excuse good enough to hurt your own child."

I met her kind eyes, shining with empathy and concern. Tears welled in my own, finally letting those words that I'd often found myself debating internally ring true.

"He brought me into this world to restore the fae to their rightful place." My voice was barely a whisper on the wind as I shared about my past, my father, and the horrors I left behind. "He had practically nothing left when he went into hiding, just a handful of his guards and a few remaining members of his court. Somehow he devised a plan to bring me into this world, killing whoever my mother had been in the process." I paused, shuddering slightly at the idea of my mother being used in such a vile manner. "I think he expected me to be a male, an heir he'd be proud to call his own... When I wasn't—well, that just made him push me harder."

I let my hands fall to my lap, allowing the wool blanket to fall with them to reveal the other markings covering my back. Luna stifled a gasp, no doubt taken aback by the sheer amount of scars marring my skin—grotesque echoes of the countless nights I spent beneath his blade. He'd spent so much time carving me into the fae he wanted for a daughter, so much time experimenting with magically embedded weapons and old fae rituals. While to most mortals the scars may appear faint, I was certain Luna understood what even the faintest scar meant on fae skin. For a fae to have any scars at all, well that was just a testament to the amount of pain they endured.

"He began training me far before I ever came into my powers, before my body had truly formed the ability to heal itself. And what little bit it did heal, he'd just reopen them again and again. He'd call me the light for our people. Just so long as he could make me strong enough."

I wanted to share more, wanted to tell her about the horrible things he did to me, the things he made me do during all of those "lessons" over the decades. But finally speaking aloud about the things I knew they already suspected, it felt like a huge step. This was my way of opening the door to that darkness still hidden inside me—a darkness that I'd one day find the strength to share with them. She belonged to the Tribes, after all—or had at some point. I didn't want to know what she'd think of me if I admitted the harm we'd brought upon them year after year in the name of strengthening my power.

"Dreaming of him tonight... I can't help but feel like it's some sort of omen," I shared instead. "It felt different than the others. And I can't shake the presence of him in my mind." I folded my arms around myself, running my hands over the gooseflesh that pebbled against my skin as I peered out into the darkness surrounding the cottage.

Luna reached out, draping the blanket back over my shoulders and handing me my cup of tea. "Drink," she ordered softly. "It will help settle your nerves. Drink and do not dwell on that monster for another moment. You're safe here." Her words were kind, but I could sense the anger seeping into her voice. While I was grateful she understood, this was part of why I'd never opened up. I didn't want Luna's peaceful spirit wasted on thoughts of that monster either. And part of me hoped if I never spoke the nightmare out loud, he'd never be able to infect the haven I'd found here.

"Thank you for trusting me enough to share, Aerie. I'm so sorry for everything you had to go through." She pulled her chair up beside mine and wrapped her arm around me. I leaned into her embrace, resting my head against her shoulder. We sat like that, staring out into the night as we let the rage and pain saturate us. My pain was her pain, and hers was mine. It was a silent ritual to affirm our bond, that we had each other no matter what, that we felt what the other was feeling no matter how painful.

I knew this because it was the same thing I'd done each time I'd learned of my sisters' stories. They had been to the Depths and back, had seen and experienced truly vile deeds in their lifetime. Every time I thought about it, it made my blood boil. Every time I silently vowed to myself that it would stop here. I would use what power my father had forced upon me to protect them, to fight for them.

Luna's soft voice rose into the night as she began singing in another language I recognized from lessons in my youth, a chant of peace and healing. I could feel her power growing with each line of the song, enveloping us in a soft, warm haze.

Perhaps I deserved some of the nightmares—after all, I wasn't entirely innocent. My hands were stained red, too. But my sisters were the embodiment of kindness and love. They were innocent and broken, and deserved protection. While we hid in this little corner of the world, I would stand guard and make sure none of them ever felt that pain again. They were my family now, and I would use every drop of my shame-filled power to protect them—no matter the cost.

CHAPTER 5
AERIE

There was a market only half a day's walk from our cottage, a small village that gathered together once or twice a month to sell handmade and homegrown goods to those of us who lived on the outskirts of the Tribes' borders. Not wanting to bring any unwanted attention to the coven due to my fae bloodline, I usually stayed home on the days that my sisters went to the market, finding ways to preoccupy myself while they were gone.

My sisters had left early that morning, before the sun was up, so that they could make it back by sundown. They had been long gone by the time I awoke, leaving me in the quiet of the cozy cottage for the day. I normally relished this time to myself, but today felt different. The dream about my father from the previous night had stirred something within me, left me feeling uneasy. Something inside me kept whispering, telling me to not let this go. Telling me that the dream had been some sort of an omen. I found myself pacing the cottage and chewing nervously on my lip, letting that singular thought turn over and over in my mind.

After a lunch of leftover soup and day-old bread, I decided staying cooped up in the cottage all by myself was making me go insane. Maybe what I needed was some time out in nature, with fresh air in my lungs and soil between my toes. I wrapped my knit shawl around my shoulders, grabbed Flora's foraging basket and notebook, and made my way out into the Dark Woods.

My thoughts elsewhere, I wandered deeper and deeper amongst the trees. I made sure to follow the path marked out by Flora's notes. The Dark Woods were an eerie place to be, predators lurking in every shadow. But I'd been sure to grab a protection bundle before making my way into the looming hemlocks. I reached into the satchel around my waist, clutching the bundle to make sure it was still there. The weight of it in my hand soothed me, causing me to pause and take a deep breath.

I needed to settle my nerves. This was nothing to lose my mind over—just old spirits haunting me. I fumbled through Flora's notebook full of sketches she'd made of plants that grew in this area, details of their benefits and where they typically grew. I'd learned so much from her in our time together, including how dangerous it could be to forage plants that you couldn't identify. I flipped through the pages as I padded through the trees, keeping an eye out for any plants that resembled those in her drawings. Before long, I'd filled my basket with sweet woodruff, lemon balm, and a healthy bundle of mint. I'd even found a peaceful spot to sit and rest in the afternoon sun streaming through a break in the canopy, enjoying the sounds of the woods and snacking on some wild berries I'd stumbled upon.

By the time I made my way back to the cottage, my mind had cleared and my body hummed with the energy of a successful forage. My sisters should have returned by now, as the sun too low in the sky for them to have still been out. I couldn't wait to show them the basket of herbs I'd collected after hearing all about their day at the market. I could always count on Esme to bring back some little luxury for us to try together, whether it be a fresh supply of bath salts or a baked sweet of some sort that she always insisted on splitting with me.

I felt a smile slip across my face, thinking on the simplicity of the life I'd found for myself here. My sisters. My home. How had I gotten so lucky to have found them? It was something I hoped I'd never take for granted—not just their love and acceptance, but this place too. This little hidden corner of the woods that felt so safe and peaceful. Even in the Dark Woods, we'd managed to carve out a safe space for each other, a life of peace and harmony. Despite everything we had overcome and even the things we still navigated together, this was our sacred space.

I stopped just short of the tree line, seeing the whimsy of our cottage peeking through the trees, glowing in the golden haze of the setting sun. I huffed out a laugh, appreciating the serenity it offered. Smoke billowed out of the chimney, letting me know that the girls had returned and were busily preparing supper. The entire scene almost felt like a mirage, a picture from a storybook that was too good to be true. I let my eyes linger a moment longer before cocking my head to the side.

The entire view flickered—an image too perfect, slipping slightly to give way to the reality behind it. The basket fell from my grasp as my hands shot to my mouth in horror, realizing finally what this was: a glamor to draw me in, faltering only once I'd come close enough to see the destruction hidden beneath it. I knew instantly who had the power to cast a glamor that strong, who would be trying to pull me in with a false sense of hope, only to crush it the moment I stepped through the door. Without a moment's hesitation, I ran up the steps.

I tripped over the rubble as I stepped through the glamor, seeing for the first time the true extent of the damage to my home. The door hung off its hinges, scorched in black marks and bubbling paint but hiding my view of the rest of the cottage. I closed my eyes, taking a deep breath even as my hands moved forward pushed against the still hot wood to reveal the horrors within.

Gone.

Everything—gone.

I stood in the entrance of the cottage, overlooking what remained of the sitting room and kitchen. Furniture had been thrown about, wrecked and splintered in whatever fight or fit of rage had taken place here. Smoke poured from still burning piles of rubble around me. The sun streamed in through holes in the roof and walls, the cottage frame still barely standing in the midst of such utter destruction.

A scream ripped from my lungs, as I burst through the smoldering remnants of the cottage. Hot, angry tears ran down my cheeks, my skin stinging with the ash and heat in the stifling air.

I tried frantically to cover my mouth, the thick air stinging my lungs as I breathed it in. The world turned upside down as I tried to make sense of what I was seeing. The smoke was consuming, blocking my view and forcing me to venture deeper into the cottage. I turned, taking in every inch of the remnants of my home, the walls crumbling even as I stood there. I attempted to find anything salvageable, anything to cling to as I felt my last thread of sanity torn to ribbons.

"No, no, no." My voice sounded distant, not connected to what my mind was processing. It wouldn't let me piece together the signs of what had happened here. My body was reacting, but my mind was three steps behind, wading through an ocean of disbelief and delusion. My gaze swept to the kitchen on the left, the dinner table nothing more than a pile of splintered, blackened wood. No one stood at the sink, washing vegetables for the supper we should be about to eat. I searched the rest of the cottage in a crazed frenzy, my desperation becoming stronger as I prayed to not find any sign of my sisters amongst the rubble that was left.

That's when my eyes landed on the bodies by the hearth—one after another piled up, scorched husks of the beings they used to be. I threw myself across the room, dropping to my knees beside them. Amidst the burnt rubble of the sitting room, I couldn't even decipher what I was looking at, *whose* bodies lay here or how many of them had met this cruel fate. Everything was cloaked in the ashen black marks of fire, their bodies lost amongst the piles of wood and stone and broken glass. I knew, though. I knew without a shadow of a doubt it was them. No one else had ever entered our cottage, we had no one to call on us or visit us here. And there were too many bodies for it to be anyone else.

My mind went to a distant place: memories of us sitting around this same hearth, sharing stories and laughing into the early hours of the morning. How many times had we gathered here, cried here? How many times had I sat amongst my sisters by this fire and thanked the Fates for the life they had given me? I was in two worlds simultaneously, watching both realities play out in my mind—experiencing the horror of this moment while trying desperately to escape to that past life. The idea of them no longer in this world broke something within me, tearing me apart until there was nothing left to put back together.

My own savage cries echoed around me, my throat raw with the pain tearing through my body. This wasn't real—this couldn't be happening. It must be some cruel trick, a glamor or a ruthless spell. But as I let my eyes fall to a hand peeking out from the smoldering mess, black and crisp from the flames that had torn through skin and muscle yet still adorned with the jade ring that Luna always wore, I knew there was no denying it. A guttural wail escaped my throat, a new wave of ravaged cries expelling from me as my stomach turned.

I imagined the pain they must have felt, the fear raging through them in their final moments—Flora and Luna succumbing to the same fate as the parents they loved so much. Esme and Serafina finally feeling safe from their pasts, only to meet a horrific fate. The sight of that delicate hand, mangled and charred even as it reached out in desperation during their final moments... I bent over, clinging to its remnants and screaming into the void that their absence had left in my soul.

My sisters. My home. Ripped from me in the most sadistic way.

I sensed a presence step out of the shadows behind me just as a rough hand wrapped around my neck. Magic—cold, black tendrils dipped in gilded poison—sank into my body. It snaked its way through me, igniting every scar that it had previously left on my skin. The rage boiling my blood burned hotter than the pain he caused, and I refused to give him the benefit of seeing my reaction. I bit down on my tongue to kill the screams fighting to break free. He'd found me. Despite how far I ran or how deep I hid, he found me. Something told me he'd always find me, that he'd never stop chasing no matter how far I ran from his grasp. And if what he'd done here today was any indication, he'd stop at nothing to have me back within his control.

"Hello, Father." My voice was rough with wicked hate and promised vengeance.

"Hello, my little light."

Before I could fight my way out of his reach, he threw me backwards. My back slammed against the stone floor, a blinding heat shooting through my body as my vision went white. I tried to fight through it, tried to scramble away, but it was no use. He was on me in an instant. I looked up to see the familiar insanity that haunted my dreams. His ice-blue eyes blazed with a frigid kind of hatred, something from the Depths itself. His stark white hair had grown feral over the years, hanging over the hollows of his cheeks in frenzied strands and draping his face in shadows. The corner of his lips ticked up, the way they always had when he reveled in my pain. He pulled a dagger from his sheath, infusing the blade with his own magic before caressing the side of my face with the heated metal.

I cried out, no longer in control of my reactions. The breath in my lungs was gone, replaced with the ashes of my home—my family—and I couldn't get down enough air to stop the trembling in my limbs.

"Did you really think you could get away from me, Aermidh? You think I would *let* you get away after everything I've poured into making you what you are?" His words were crazed, their weight striking a fever pitch within me. "I've been watching you since you left my care, sweet child, waiting for the perfect moment to swoop in and return you to your rightful place."

Nausea swirled in my gut, fear creeping into every pore of my body. I'd somehow convinced myself that I'd been safe here, that I could protect them and myself from the insanity of this male. How had I been so delusional? My jaw quivered as I turned my head back towards the hearth to the mangled bodies that had once been my sisters.

"Why would you do this?" I asked in a whisper, vicious tears spilling down my face. My father's gaze followed mine as he tsked.

"Imagine my disappointment—my *disgust*—as I realized this is what you left our home behind for." He spat in their direction, cursing into the thick smoky air. "Witches, Aermidh? Members from the *tribes*? How dare you defile your power with those har-lots!"

"Those females had more strength than you could even fath-om," I spat back, writhing beneath his grasp, desperate to fight for the family he stole from me. I kicked out, trying to get my legs between us to pry him off of me.

"Ah, ah, ah." He pressed the dagger into my throat, pinning me beneath the blade.

"Do it!" I cried out. "Do it and be done with it. I'd rather die than go back to that prison you call a home."

I didn't care if he killed me. Without my sisters, I had nothing to live for. And I would die before letting him take me captive again.

Something in his eye glimmered, his need to inflict pain calling out for the kill. He let the blade slice into my skin, dragging it down my neck. Blood pooled along my chest, but even as I screamed at the pain his blade caused me, I knew he was holding back.

Sheathing the blade, he dipped his fingers in my blood and began drawing symbols in our ancient fae language against my chest. With each marking, I felt my power drain. I thrashed, desperate to be free of his hold—willing my magic to over-power him. Even as I desperately clung to it, I felt the moment the last hint of it slipped away, laying dormant within me and leaving me completely at his mercy.

"I know you don't understand the things I've made you do, Aermidh." His bloody fingers stroked the side of my face as I pulled away, trying to dodge the sickening feel of his touch. "The things I've done for you. But it is all for your good, my little light. All for the good of our people."

I spat in his face as he leaned in, watching with satisfaction as he wiped a hand over his eyes in disgust. "Fuck your people," I hissed. "I want nothing to do with your kingdom or you."

He sighed, disappointment washing over his features. "Yes, you've made that abundantly clear." He gestured around the ashen wreckage of the cottage and shook his head, letting it drop over me. "I had such high hopes for you, Aermidh." Something like grief flitted across his eyes, catching me off guard before he continued: "But alas, we've reached a bit of a predicament, my sweet girl."

My brow furrowed as I watched him, my body feeling utterly helpless even as it begged to break free of the wards he'd put on me.

"You see, you have defiled yourself with this foolish meddling. Our people will no longer accept you." He cocked his head to the side, tightening his grip as he debated over his words. "*I will no longer accept you.*"

His words shouldn't have hurt, I didn't want anything to do with his wicked plans. I didn't need his acceptance. Still, I froze as they washed over me. Somewhere deeper, a primal desire was extinguished. A long-lasting hope that perhaps one day he'd see me as his daughter, not a tool to further his kingdom, or a vessel for his rage.

"All those lessons I imparted on you left you a weapon too powerful to let go. But your meddling in this disgraceful magic has left you too defiled to be of any use to me." He sucked in a long, deep breath, his nostrils flaring in irritation.

The last remnants of sunset streamed in through the gaping holes in the cottage walls that his wrath had left behind. The familiar orange haze lit up the room, the smoke clearing just enough for me to imagine what it would have looked like to come home one more time. The memory of what I'd lost renewed my anger, my fight, and I took the opportunity to lash out. My fist landed squarely against his jaw, but his warding had weakened my body. The motion barely impacted him as he raised his arm, backhanding me. I stifled a sob, blood trickling down my face. He ran a hand through his long, untamed, hair, the white strands now speckled with my blood and the ashes falling around us like a first winter's snow.

Tendrils of his magic snaked and tightened across my skin, sending a bone-chilling dread down my spine and throughout my body even as I fought harder to break free.

"No, no, *please*!" I screamed. "Don't do this!" No words felt desperate enough, already knowing that begging would get me nowhere.

Binding me beneath him, he looked down on me with a mixture of disgust and disappointment. He held up his hand, letting the darkness of his magic swirl between each finger. My entire body shook as I fought against the bindings.

"I had great plans for you, Aermidh. You were to be the rebirth of our people. But if this is the path you choose, then I won't allow that power to fall to anyone else. I won't take your magic. I don't want it now that it's *tainted*. But I will make damn sure you can't pass on the power I've cultivated in you."

I could barely hear him over the panic of my own pleas, barely caught sight of his intent as he ran his hands over my skin, brushing my hair out of my face and tracing the wound he'd cut into me. The haunting, familiar chill of his touch—of his magic—stung like ice as I clawed desperately at the wooden floor beneath my fingers. I felt my nails splinter, felt my skin break as my own blood pooled around me. But the pain didn't even register as my desperation to get away from him grew. This pain was nothing compared to what I knew he'd inflict on me.

Ripping at the fabric of my dress and exposing my body, he sat back and took in the sight of my bare, burning skin—the edges of the scars he'd carved into me peeking around my sides. My stomach turned, my muscles fighting to cover myself. His eyes widened as I trembled. He ran his bony fingers over the thick ridges of my scars, admiring his work. It felt like time itself paused as I lay frozen beneath him, watching helplessly as he relished in this moment with a twisted sort of enthusiasm. Something wicked glimmered in his eye as he flattened his hand against my abdomen. The fear ravaging my body as I squirmed and thrashed was a stark contrast to the unnerving calm that overtook him.

"I'm sorry, my little light," he whispered through a sinister grin as he allowed his magic to slowly sink into my skin, my muscle, until it crept deeper and cut like a knife at the organs within. Blinding pain shot through me as I felt his magic take hold of my body, my future, tearing it to shreds within me. Pain like I'd never experienced tore through me, pulling me under and extinguishing the light that I'd worked so hard to build back up within myself. Within an instant he'd stolen everything from me—my family, my power, my choice, and my future.

Tears blurred my vision as they fell freely down my cheeks, my fight bleeding out. My head rolled to the side as the pain threatened to take over. My father was speaking, but I couldn't understand the words, his sounds blending together into a distant buzzing that I tried desperately to drown out with my own sobs. I let my gaze focus on the hand sticking out of the pile by the hearth, forcing my mind to wander to those perfect nights beneath the moon, dancing in the joy of my sisters. My father might rip me apart, but my mind would be with them, holding my peace even in my last moments. Something I couldn't do for them. Their spirits were still here, holding my hand as I faded away, letting my father slice into me and cut out every good thing I'd finally found for myself.

CHAPTER 6
BASTIAN

The Dark Woods were my least favorite place amongst the Tribes. I would never understand why my brother insisted on spending his time beneath the canopy of its shadows. The trees stretched and groaned with every one of my motions, as if they watched in patient observation. The Dark Woods harbored an ancient kind of magic, one that predated even the Old Magic of the damned fae rule. This was a different kind of magic, a kind I didn't fully understand, and therefore didn't trust.

Which begged me to reason why I was dragging my ass out here to look for my brother. If he was foolish enough to get himself killed out here, then I knew I should just let him find that fate. I grumbled to myself as I tracked the cloud of thick black smoke hanging above the trees on the quickly dimming horizon. It had been weeks since he'd returned to the estate, and no matter how little I cared to admit it, I'd started venturing out into the Dark

Woods for any sign of him. I knew I'd never be able to actually leave him to the consequences of his actions. We'd already lost too much.

Vander had always had a habit for getting into trouble—a short temper and a large reputation for overreacting—but he'd been a completely different person since we lost Hazlenn. I paused, leaning against the bark of a hemlock as I wiped my brow and adjusted my axes. Even the thought of her name brought trepidation to my gut. I wasn't sure what was a worse fate, being dead or being in the hands of Kahlis, and it was driving me mad trying to determine which outcome I'd rather Vander find. I assumed that's what he was doing out here, not that he'd actually taken the time to explain to me where he was going on his endless nights away.

Thankfully he'd stopped long enough to transfer the title of chieftain to me, leaving me to clean up the mess he'd made out of our tribe. Our borders were in shreds, the warding practically nonexistent. Our tribe members were scared out of their wits with the threat of Kahlis' kingdom ever encroaching on us, especially now that Vander had left the tribe unprotected. I couldn't even be mad at him, though; I was barely in a better place myself. First our parents, now Hazlenn. It was starting to feel incredibly lonely at the estate, the small family who had once surrounded us snuffed out the longer this battle with Kahlis went on.

But my title of chieftain at least offered me some level of protection within these woods. It might be an old kind of magic that lurked here, but it seemed to hold at least some kind of respect for our world's power. Perhaps it recognized strength and honor amongst those who walked through these trees. I shifted uncomfortably, suddenly realizing that perhaps the trees were watching to assess if I was worthy enough to pass.

Finally, the trees began to thin and the thick smell of smoke and decay stung my nostrils, causing my steps to slow as my eyes searched the wreckage for any threat. I could make out a small cottage just ahead, apparently the source of the haze that was now seeping into the Dark Woods. I lifted my tunic to my mouth, using the fabric to protect from the scent of scorched flesh and dark magic hanging heavy in the air.

By the time I reached the steps to the cottage, it was clear to see that whatever evil had caused this was long gone. Flames no longer licked at the walls, or what was left of them. Embers glowed in the piles of rubble around the remains of the cottage, steadily smoldering as I carefully stepped through them. No signs of Vander—at least that much was a relief. I hated myself for even thinking it, but there were no signs of Hazlenn either. Even if it was insane to still search for her any time I ventured out of the estate, it was an impulse I couldn't quell.

The truth of the matter was that these instances had become ever more frequent with the current state of our tribe. Those on the outskirts of the tribe's borders were at a higher risk for attacks and I'd found myself too often as of late, wandering out into the Dark Woods to stumble upon the remnants of such atrocities—looking for survivors and doing what I could as chieftain to lessen the impact of these attacks against our tribe.

I made my way over to the hearth, following the source of the stench. I cringed as I saw the remains lying there, too mangled and burnt to even identify. I understood why some desired to live a life of seclusion. It was a choice I respected, but it was impossible to offer them protection outside of the tribe's borders. Unfortunately, this wasn't all that uncommon of a tragedy to find. I turned away from the bodies, sending out a silent death prayer for them as I let my eyes skim the rest of the rubble for any survivors.

My eyes caught on another form off to the side. I hadn't noticed it at first, mistaking it for just another pile of rubble. But something low in my gut was pushing me toward it. My footsteps echoed through the empty space as I dropped beside the pile of dirtied sheets. I let go of the tunic covering my face, freeing my hands to inspect the odd bundle. Pulling back the sheets, I stumbled backwards in shock. Beneath the bloodstained and ashen cotton fabric was another body, not burned like the rest but stripped bare, badly beaten, and bleeding. Her eyes were closed, long almost white tresses unfurling around the disturbed sheets and tattered fabric. Her long lashes were dusted with ash, her alabaster skin splattered with blood and muck from the destruction surrounding her.

I quickly pressed my fingers to her neck, checking for a pulse. To my relief, there was a slow but steady rhythm. I moved the debris around her, giving myself room to carefully pick her up and get her out of the haunting remnants of this house. I eased her into my arms, taking care not to touch any of the visible wounds on her fragile body and covering her in one of the sheets. A string of garbled words and moans escaped her, her head lobbing to the side as she sank back into unconsciousness.

"Fucking Fates," I muttered, looking down at the very pointed ear sticking out between matted strands of bloodstained blonde hair. What the fuck was a *fae* doing this close to the tribe's border?

I hesitated for a moment. I knew what I had to do, but it went against what I knew I *should* do as chieftain. My first priority needed to be the safety of my tribe. The fae were a violent breed. They had done so much damage to our tribe—my family. We had too much on our plates to get involved in another fae battle. I knew what Vander would do if he were the one here. He would walk away—wouldn't dare to bring a fae over the tribe's borders. He'd say the risk was too high. But was it enough to abandon a helpless female and leave her for dead amongst this wreckage?

Looking down at the helpless form in my arms, at the violence she'd so clearly endured, I couldn't find it in me to leave her amongst the burning remnants of the cottage. I might not have been able to save the others, but she was still here—still alive. I owed it to her and myself to at least get her out of here.

"Fuck." I ground my teeth together, turning away from the embers of the still burning wreckage. I already knew this was a mistake. With every step I took back into the Dark Woods, my body was screaming at me to leave her. But something deeper was stirring, something I couldn't quite explain. And I'd be damned if I'd see any more death around me.

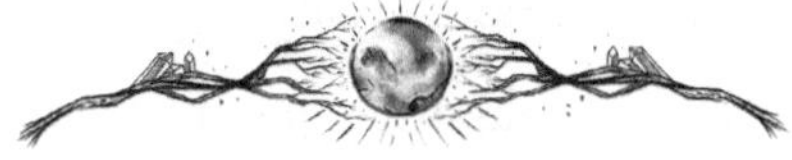

I made my way back through the Dark Woods and towards the estate. I let some of my wolven features slip into place, replacing my vision with my other form and allowing my sight to heighten in the darkness of the night. The trees ahead came into focus, the woods beyond them becoming clearer as I searched the night for any predators lurking. Moonlight leaked through the treetops, falling on the female and casting her in a pure silver glow as I monitored her breathing. As we ventured closer to the estate, her breaths quickened. Her moans peppered the night's air as she stirred, slowly slipping back into consciousness.

I stopped beside a nearby hemlock, removing my cloak to allow her some cushion as I laid her against the trunk. Her eyes rolled as she came to, her body going rigid with fear as she met my gaze.

"Easy now," I murmured in a low tone, trying to make my voice as calm and nonthreatening as possible. She sat upright at my words, immediately crying out at the pain brought on by the sudden motion.

"Who are you?" she croaked out, her throat no doubt raw from the amount of smoke she'd inhaled at that cottage. "Where am I?"

"Just take it easy, okay? You're safe, I'm not going to hurt you."

Her eyes darted nervously around us. Her body was shaking as she no doubt tried to wrap her mind around what was happening.

"My name is Bastian," I said, laying a hand on my chest. "I'm Chieftain of the Tribe of Talamh." I pulled at the sleeve of my tunic, showing her the elemental markings on my arm—a web of dark earthy roots winding down my forearm. I wasn't sure if they'd mean anything to her. Judging by the look of confusion and fear on her face, I supposed not.

"I found you in a burned down cottage a ways off from here. I'm just trying to take you home so we can clean you up and get you the help you need."

Her eyes went wide, her head shaking in fierce rejection.

"I can't cross into the Tribe's borders," she argued, genuine fear etched into her features.

"Did someone from Talamh do this to you?" Anger rose involuntarily in my blood. My people were scared, sure, but this was an unacceptable evil. I wouldn't stand for my tribe partaking in such a vicious attack. She just kept shaking her head, refusing to answer my question.

"You'll be safe with me at my estate, I promise. You can leave as soon as you are in better shape. But we have to get you out of the Dark Woods and start tending to your wounds." Her vision still shifted around us, looking for any nearby threat, or possibly a way to escape. I reached out a hand, trying to steady her shaking, but she jumped at my motion and I put my hands up as a show of surrender. "You can trust me, I promise. I'm not going to harm you. I just want to help."

She took several steadying breaths, nodding at last. I moved to pick her up again, but she pushed me back, hard—knocking me on my ass.

"I can walk." The words rushed out of her in one heavy breath. I paused, giving her the space to realize for herself that she definitely could not walk on her own. She pushed off the ground once, twice, before falling back in an exhale of defeat. At last, she allowed me to approach again, slipping an arm over my shoulder as I guided her to her feet.

It was dangerous to bring a fae here. I was barely managing to keep my calm, but I didn't really see an alternative. I couldn't leave her out here, especially not in the state she was in. As I watched her struggle to get to her feet, I knew I had to hold it together a little longer.

Even in this close proximity, I could feel her hesitance to lean on me, to trust me. I had to admire her caution. She was a fighter, I'd give her that much. She had to be in a massive amount of pain, not to mention spooked out of her mind. But whether it was shock or strength that spurred her forward, she moved nonetheless. I gritted my teeth as we trudged forward, my eyes turning upward to the looming hemlocks as they watched the fae cross over the tribe's borders—being led by none other than the Chieftain.

CHAPTER 7
AERIE

The shifter led us back through the woods, his wolven eyes peering out into the darkness of the Dark Woods as we made our way back to his home. It was impossible to miss what his magic was; he reeked of dog, and just being near him made my stomach turn. Or perhaps that was the pain ravaging my body with each step I took. Maybe it would have been better to just let him carry me, but I refused to be at the mercy of another male. I didn't trust him, no matter how pure he promised his intentions to be. I preferred to have a chance to run if he decided to deceive me.

As we walked, I assessed my wounds as best I could, wiping away the wardings marked in my own blood, by my father's hand. It was a momentary relief, feeling the power of my magic slip back in place and seep into the already healing wounds. Still, it would take time to truly heal them, if I could at all. My father's magic was powerful, and bile rose in my throat as I felt it lying deep within me—hiding and twining through my own.

We eventually arrived at a vast estate standing tall and unkind against the late-night glow of the moon—as if all sense of home and comfort had been drained from it some time ago, leaving it abandoned and barren. No light flickered within the structure and I found my gut twisting in apprehension as we approached, the sight too similar to the prison my father kept me in for so long. I shouldn't be here, shouldn't be trusting this mysterious creature who was leading me into unknown territory.

We had to be within the Tribes borders by now, somewhere I very much tried to avoid being. Their people were unkind to beings like me, beings of Old Magic. I twisted back towards the woods we'd just come from, wondering if it was too late to run, too late to go back to the embers of my home.

But it didn't matter if I could get away; nothing was left for me there now.

The shifter watched me through guarded eyes as he pushed me forward and ushered me through a side entrance, taking a long look beyond me into the woods before shutting the door with a firm sort of finality.

"Here," he grumbled as he pulled out a stool for me and guided me onto the seat.

He fumbled around a room that appeared to be a large kitchen, cursing under his breath as he raided the nearby shelves in the darkness. He then moved to the far wall, leaning over the hearth. Within moments, a fire blazed to life. He didn't linger long, though, as he continued digging through cupboards and cabinets, looking for what, I did not know.

Eventually he found what he was looking for and pulled his own stool up beside me, keeping a noticeable distance from my reach, as he set two glasses down in front of us and a bottle of some darkened liquid. He uncorked the bottle, swiftly pouring a glass for me and then himself. Setting the bottle down with more force than necessary, he lifted his glass, anxious to suck down whatever spirits he'd been so desperate to find. His eyes caught mine momentarily, assessing my pointed refusal to touch the glass. He stayed there a moment, glass raised in the air, waiting for me to join him.

"Suit yourself," he said, throwing back his glass and then reaching to swipe mine away and downed that too. I scoffed, the motion inflaming the wounds covering my body, lining my face, as a flash of pain ran hot through me. I winced, unable to hide the involuntary reaction, and the shifter in front of me ground his teeth at the noise.

I wrapped my arms around myself, desperate for some sort of reprieve from his burrowing eyes. They were the eyes of a predator, no matter if he'd helped me or not, and I wouldn't allow myself to feel safe here. This was just a temporary resting spot, somewhere to stop long enough for me to regroup and figure out what my next move was. I rubbed at my soot-covered arms subconsciously beneath the borrowed cloak, visions of the fire and anguish reigniting in my mind. I squeezed my eyes shut, face scrunching as I desperately tried to push the pain away.

Without warning, he pushed himself up off his stool, the wooden legs scraping and groaning against the kitchen floor. The noise was too loud for the quiet of the house and I suddenly found my panic rising at the thought of who he'd alert to our presence with all of his commotion. I assumed others were here; it seemed too big a house for him to occupy on his own. He stormed through the doorway into the next room and I found myself leaning ever so slightly in an attempt to watch what he was doing. He returned momentarily with a large wool blanket.

"Here." He stuck his arm out, shoving the blanket towards me. My mouth fell open in surprise. For someone who was practically a wild animal, he was acting rather kind. Or at least, was trying to. It was hard to miss the disdain on his face as he dropped the blanket, ensuring not to get too close as I took it from him. He went back to searching through cabinets, pulling out a small vial or two and setting them on the counter between us. I wrapped the thick material around me and instantly sank into the comfort it provided. Finally relaxing a bit, I wiped my hands over my dirty and bloodied face in an effort to cleanse myself, wincing again as I hit the angry wounds. I pushed my hair out of my eyes, trying to tame the wild tresses by tucking them behind my ears.

It was impossible to miss the way he blatantly stared at them as he worked, the one obvious tell of my fae heritage. There were many other ways to spot a fae, but I was sure this brutelike shifter wouldn't be able to point out any of them. I ground my teeth together as I settled back into my seat, pulling the blanket tighter and cherishing the false sense of safety it provided.

The firelight finally gave me the opportunity to notice the shifter's features. His chestnut hair had been pulled back at some point, but loose strands now framed his face and brushed his shoulders. His eyes were molten honey, the rich browns swirling with the accent of the dancing flames reflecting in them. Despite his broad frame, his face looked hollow, sunken, as if he hadn't had a good night's sleep in quite some time. He slowed his motions, noticing the way I was cautiously watching him. He held my gaze for several long moments, whatever salves and medicines in his hands suddenly forgotten.

The shifter finally shook his head, letting his gaze fall as he let out a long sigh.

"Look, I—" The door to the kitchen burst open, cutting him off from whatever he'd been about to say. I jumped, expecting the worst as I spun to face the doorway and fight the evil that had followed us here. How had he found me again? My eyes went blind with fear—a steady high-pitched ringing splitting through my ears as I readied myself to fight.

Instead of my father's bitter, hate-filled face, I found the darkened eyes of another mysterious monster. When he entered the room, it was as if all life were being sucked out of it. A chill settled over my skin as I cowered away from his presence. I didn't know what his magic was, but it had my own screaming to run far, far away.

He stalked forward, not initially noticing my presence as he made to push past the other male. I held my breath as he stopped short, his nostrils flaring as he caught my scent. I stilled in fear as his eyes finally found mine.

"Bastian," the male called out in a low rumble. The temperament of his words had me praying to the gods long forgotten. "What the *fuck* is a fae female doing in our kitchen?"

I'd been so distracted by this male's presence that I hadn't even noticed the way the shifter who'd found me had carefully stepped between us, hands up as if he was talking down a bloodthirsty animal.

"Vander, let me explain. Everything is fine, no one is in danger."

"Everything is not *fine*." Ice crusted the air as he spoke. "And *someone* is most definitely in danger." He prowled forward, not even the least bit deterred by the male between us. His eyes were too dark, the same raven hue as the hair that clung wildly around his face. He looked feral, unruly—unpredictable and terrifying with the way the moonlight streaming in through the open door backlit his tall form. I understood his threat immediately. Any other day, I would have stood my ground, welcomed the fight, and returned the heat with as much ferocity as he was giving. But today? Today I barely had the strength to stand, let alone take on the dark magic that now filled the other half of the kitchen.

"Stand down, brother," the shifter warned through gritted teeth. My eyes bounced from one brute to the other, trying to understand the dynamic—the threat. Did he say *brother*? The monster in front of me looked so different—so otherworldly—to be the shifter's brother. His magic was different, darker. The dark one moved to strike, cutting me off from fully assessing the difference between them. Before I could catch my breath he had me pinned against the wall, a blade against my throat, and the other shifter attempting to pull him off me.

Within an instant, I was back in the cottage, back beneath the mercy of my father. Visions swarmed in my mind; instead of this strange shifter, I saw my father in front of me, holding a similar blade against me, just as he had only a few hours ago. My chin quivered, reality blending into the nightmares that plagued me.

"We don't allow fae filth in these lands," the shifter hissed, the heat of his breath filling my face. I blinked, the image of my father fading, as his words sank in. He tightened his grip on the blade, pressing it deeper against my skin. I felt the swift sting as blood trickled down my chest. But what was one more nick amongst the multitude of scars I bore? He leaned in close as he let his hate-filled threat roll off his tongue.

"You were a fool to come here, and you will pay with your life."

CHAPTER 8
BASTIAN

I steadied my hand against my brother's shoulder, putting as much power behind the motion as I felt safe using in such close proximity to the female beneath his blade. His rage was unmatched these days, constantly at the surface and threatening to explode. In many ways, I didn't blame him. We'd been through so much in recent years—and losing Hazlenn was a blow I wasn't sure either of us would ever recover from.

"Vander." My voice was calm, resolute, as I urged him to step down. He didn't so much as budge, causing a tremor to run down my spine as I felt his shadows surge around the kitchen. He was so different now, so much harder than the brother I grew up with. I barely recognized him anymore. He refused to talk about it, but it was impossible to miss the changes in his magic since Hazlenn's disappearance. It was somehow darker—more violent—and accompanied by these ever-present shadows that seemed to stem from something vile inside him. I couldn't tell if it was just the loss weighing on him, or something else entirely that now influenced his unhinged behavior.

It had been weeks since I'd seen him, months since he'd been home or checked in. He was off doing Fates knew what in the Dark Woods, hunting down Hazlenn or Kahlis or maybe just anything that moved. I had never been great at connecting with my brother before, but now... now it felt impossible to break through that wall of shadowed darkness he'd built around himself.

I tightened my grip on his shoulder, refusing to let him hurt this female further. Yes, she was fae. And yes, it made my skin crawl seeing her in our family's estate after everything the fae had taken from us. So much of our family's—our tribe's—blood had been spilled at the hands of Khalis, one of the exiled fae kings. We were in a never-ending war against him and his creatures, constantly fighting to keep him off of our borders and out of our villages. And now, Hazlenn was missing because of him. My parents had *died* because of him.

The fae had always had a reputation for violence and a hunger for blood, but this ongoing battle with Kahlis was just further proof of how vile the fae could be.

But the fae female in front of me was hurting—wounded and scared. He wouldn't restore any of those losses by keeping her pinned to the wall, beneath both his blade and his shadows pressing into her.

"I need to speak with you." I didn't give him a chance to argue as I turned, dragging him towards the hallway beyond the kitchen.

"*Now.*" He hesitated a moment, staring down the fae female. His eyes flicked to the wound across her chest, reopened and bleeding once again, before backing away slowly and following me down the hallway. Even without his presence against her, she didn't move from her spot. I clenched my jaw as I realized he'd left his shadows pressed against her in an effort to hold her in place.

I let out a frustrated sigh as I rubbed my thumb and fore-finger against my head, pinching my brow. "Vander, you can't just disappear for months and then storm back in here, taking control of the situation." My voice was lowered as I scolded him, trying to tamp down on the anger burning inside of me.

"Last I checked, I could do whatever I wanted. And if I think the leader of this tribe should know better than to let a fae into our borders, I'll make my point clear."

I bit back my retort, suppressing the urge to scoff at his opinions on leadership. His role as chieftain had been a joke. Leaders didn't run in times of turmoil. Leaders didn't disappear and leave the rest of us scrambling to pick up the slack. And that's exactly what he did, leaving me to pick up the pieces since he'd been too overcome with grief or rage to step up and lead our tribe as he was duty-bound to do.

I stepped up to him, squaring my shoulders and taking a steadying breath. "You no longer lead this tribe, brother. You passed that duty to me. Now trust me to do my job."

Vander sneered as he looked me over, fortifying his stance and refusing to back down. His jaw flexed as his shadows encircled us, the muscles in his arms pulsing as he waited for me to challenge him.

I hated that this became our fight. He may have passed his title as chieftain to me, but it wasn't a decision he wanted to make. In many ways, I believed he resented me for having to do so, for seeing me in the position that was meant for him. It was not one I wanted either, but one I felt a duty to take on. Someone had to look after this tribe, especially with Kahlis circling closer than ever before.

I looked over his shoulder, eyes trained on the small amount of the female I could make out through the wake of Vander's shadows. The firelight cast a warm glow on her dirtied and bruised skin, even through the shadows pinning her down.

"She's a victim, Vander. I don't care what she is or how much we don't like her kind. She's hurt and she needs our help."

There was a beat of silence as my brother watched me, folding his arms across his chest. I couldn't tell what he was thinking, so I pressed on.

"I couldn't leave her out there to die—Fates knows what happened to her in the first place. You weren't there, Vander. You didn't see the ruins of that cottage, the wounds inflicted on her, or how scared she..." I trailed off, shaking my head as I realized there was no use reasoning with him. Her wounds had already begun healing through our journey here and no matter their depth, Vander would never sympathize for a wounded fae. I sighed deeply, rubbing at my brow to alleviate some of the tension building there. "She needs help and I was just lucky enough to be the one to find her. Perhaps if you hadn't been gallivanting through the Dark

Woods and doing fuck knows what, I wouldn't have been out there looking for you to stumble upon her."

He growled, the vibration raising the hairs on my neck, but I stood my ground.

"What would mother do?" I challenged. "She wouldn't have even questioned bringing her in to help. You know that."

"Mother's generosity is what got her killed in the first place."

I clenched my jaw, hating how he talked about her death in such a way. "And I'm certain you turning out to be a bitter, callous shifter is exactly what she sacrificed her life for." I spit back, shutting him up. Though anger broiled in his eyes, he finally stepped away, releasing his shadows from the female as he did.

"Fine," he bit out. "She stays only long enough to heal. Then I will personally escort her across the border." He turned back to the kitchen, making his way back outside. He paused as he passed her, throwing her a disdainful look. "Try anything while you're here and I will end you before you can finish your scheming." Pure disgust dripped from him. "I know how your kind are."

He pushed past us out into the night, slamming the door hard enough to send a few of the pots on the shelves clambering to the ground. I let loose a breath, relieved to finally be free of those shadows and his judgmental eyes. He wasn't the only one who held such a hard bias against the fae, but he also wasn't the one who found her in the woods, bleeding and burning in the remnants of that cottage...

I couldn't just leave her there.

I saw something in those pain-filled eyes, something different and soft. Something that got the best of my curiosity. It was the same thing I could see now as she watched my brother storm out. She had a fierce kind of fight in her, a dangerously determined one, perhaps. But there was more that intrigued me: pain and guilt and love swirled in those bright blue eyes. Something worth saving.

Maybe I was a fool for ever giving it notice.

CHAPTER 9
AERIE

I let loose a shuddering breath as the shadows receded from the room, my legs feeling suddenly weak without the force of that *thing's* power against me. The shifter was beside me in a matter of moments, looping my arm over him and helping guide me back to my seat.

"I'm sorry about him," he grumbled. My body was shaking again, the chill in the air seeping deeper into my skin. I found myself leaning into the warmth of the fire, clutching the blanket even tighter around me as I followed his movements through heavy-lidded eyes.

"He hasn't quite been himself since—" The shifter's voice faded, his head shaking as he moved to the far side of the kitchen. "He's just going through some things right now. Still, it doesn't excuse his behavior."

"Trust me, I've experienced worse from your kind," I bit back, suddenly feeling a rush of bitterness. The tribes had always been prejudiced against the fae, it was nothing new to me. Typically, it was not something that bothered me. I more than understood their hesitancy to trust the fae, especially given the hatred that ran deep in our bloodline for any beings the Fates had gifted power to. It was a long-standing feud over power and station, one painted in bloodshed and violence. But sitting here now, broken and bleeding, I was having a hard time dismissing his intolerance and letting go of the anger.

Bastian tapped his fingers on the stone hearth where he leaned, watching me carefully. "And what are your feelings towards the tribes?" he asked finally, his eyes narrowing in assessment as he waited for my reply.

I sighed, letting the anger dissipate due to the exhaustion fighting for dominance. "I have none," I lied. "I have no thoughts for either side, no alliances with the fae or with the tribes. I—" My voice broke as the realization hit me. "I have no one."

I cleared my throat, turning my head towards the wood burning in the fireplace, refusing to say more on the matter. I could feel the shifter's eyes on me, evaluating every movement of my body for any hint of insincerity. Finally, he broke away from the hearth and bumbled around the kitchen, before setting a bowl of water and some strips of linen next to a few bottles from the hutch on the counter beside us. He stepped back with an awkward pause.

"Believe it or not, that drink I offered was for you. While you've managed to heal those wounds quite nicely on your own, they require more attention and *that* will sting. Unfortunately I , uh... don't have much on hand to help." His voice was heavy with pity as he looked down on the sparse supplies laid out across the counter. "Nor am I much skilled in using them." He chuckled slightly, the noise sounding forced and dying in the space between us. "I can call for a healer, but she probably won't be here till—"

"No," I cut him off, straightening at his words. I didn't want anyone else to know I was here. Perhaps I was safe for now, my father presumably expecting I would have died in that torment he'd left me in. He might have lost interest in me for now, but I didn't want to risk alerting others to my presence here, in case he decided to suddenly change his mind and come after me again.

"No, that won't be necessary," I added when I realized he was eying me cautiously. "I can walk you through what to do. Besides, I won't need much tending. Mostly just time to let my body heal itself."

He paused a moment longer, his gaze shifting between me and the supplies he'd laid out. "Alright," he answered at last. "Tell me what to do."

I nodded towards the strips of linen. "Grab some of those, submerge them in the water." He did as I said without a moment's hesitation. I walked him through the process of cleaning the wounds on my face and the one along my chest—the one that had reopened thanks to the force of his brother's power. His touch was gentler than I expected, given how rough his brother had been with me, and I felt myself leaning into the comforting presence of another's touch after the storm of grief and shock that had been ravaging my body.

He cleaned what little he could reach, going over each cut—each bruise—with a thick ointment that was dry and aged from what I assumed was years of being discarded in the hutch. He didn't pry, didn't ask what had caused my wounds and when he saw my hand rub absent-mindedly along my abdomen, where I could still feel the dark magic twisting inside of me like a cruel knife, he simply placed a jar of ointment in my hand.

"I can show you to one of the guest chambers, draw you a bath if you'd like? I'm afraid there's only so much I can do with this." He gestured to the now dirtied water and used linen. I glanced down, looking at my arms, my hands, the ends of my white hair now sullied with the ashes from the fire. Despite his best efforts, I was still filthy—shame and guilt burning my skin along with each streak of black. I wondered how many of the burned cinders that clung to me were the fragmented remains of my sisters.

Tears began to fall as I blinked, looking back to him and nodding my head in numb agreement. I could tell seeing the emotion caused him discomfort, as he fidgeted with his hands as he waited for me to move. When I didn't—when I couldn't—he let out a small breath, moving closer.

"Is it alright if I carry you?" he asked, leaning in and bracing himself to lift me. I couldn't bring myself to talk, to think, so instead I just nodded again and winced as he picked me up and wrapped me in his warmth. I leaned into the embrace, cherishing the warmth of this total stranger, and wondering if I had truly, finally lost my mind. More tears fell, but I couldn't help but feel safe here, like I could crumble entirely within this space and it would be okay.

He moved swiftly through the halls, leading us to some far corner of the estate. He glided like satin, careful not to disturb me, not to cause me any more pain than what I was already enduring. Eventually he made his way into a dark room, setting me down carefully in a nearby chair before retreating to the bathing chamber and running a bath. I took in the room, my head on a swivel as I looked for any other signs of life around me. The room was vacant, aside from a simple bed in the corner and the chair by the fire that I was sitting in. It was stark, but a welcome relief to not find any prying eyes or listening ears. While the tub filled, he lit a fire in the hearth and added several stones to the logs. I watched in silent observation, studying this male who had found me in the woods, in the midst of my nightmare, and brought me into his home with no questions asked.

I'd counted myself lucky to find the coven when I did, to be accepted so fully and loved so thoroughly. They took me in as family and never made me feel like anything less. It was highly improbable that this could be the same as that. The Fates showed me favor once already, why would they offer me another opportunity?

He grabbed the hot stones off the fire, adding them to the copper tub before kneeling beside my chair. If I'd had any energy left at all, I might have told him not to bother with the stones; usually, my magic could warm the water. But even if I could speak, I wasn't sure there was any power left in my magic, after how much it had been working to heal all my father had done to me.

"The bath is ready whenever you are." He spoke in a gentle whisper. "There's some extra clothes in the wardrobe when you're done. And you can sleep here tonight. My room is just across the hall if you need anything."

He patted my hand hesitantly, unsure what else to say. Within a moment, he was on his feet and striding out the door.

"Th—thank you." I barely recognized my own voice as it cracked and slipped across the room. I couldn't turn to look at him, couldn't manage anything more than those two words. He paused for a long time, so long that I wondered if he hadn't heard me and had left to his own bedchambers.

"Nothing will harm you here," he finally responded. "I give you my word."

And with that, his footsteps retreated and the door clicked shut. I let out one long, low breath, feeling the weight of all that had happened today creep out of whatever recess of my mind it was hiding in. My shoulders slumped, my gaze falling to my soiled clothing. Charred, black streaks covered my body. The smell of burnt flesh and decay clung to me. I couldn't bring myself to get in the bath, though. I couldn't bring myself to wash away the last remaining pieces of my sisters, no matter how much the realization made my stomach churn. Instead, I sat in the reach of the firelight, letting the shadow of the flames dance around me—consume me—as I buried my head in my hands and cried.

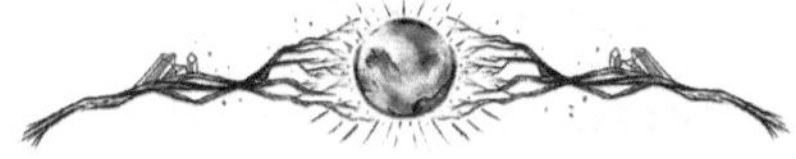

I awoke the next morning to a stack of books waiting for me, alongside a simple breakfast tray on the bedside table. My eyes were heavy, either from the lack of sleep or the amount of crying that happened the night before. It had been hours before I'd found the courage to get in the bath. Despite cleansing myself of the ash and blood that clung to me last night, the horrors of yesterday still plagued my mind—the feeling of my father's hands still lingered on my skin.

I picked at the food, trying to find something to distract myself from where my thoughts had turned. The food was not exceptionally great but mildly impressive if the shifter had been the one cooking it. I ate as much as I could stomach, but the pain weaving through my body was still causing strong bouts of nausea that I couldn't seem to shake. Pushing the tray away, I turned my attention towards the books. A knock sounded at the door as I spread the various titles out across the bed.

"I was just coming by to check on you," he offered hesitantly as he leaned against the doorframe. Even in the midst of his kindness he seemed so shy, so nervous to be around me. I dipped my head back towards the books to hide the small smile threatening to break through. It was somehow endearing, him being both equally concerned and terrified of me.

"I see you found your breakfast, and the books." He nodded towards the stack spread before me. "I thought you may need something to keep you occupied while you're holed up in bed, healing."

I opened my mouth to argue. I had no intention of staying here—let alone lying in bed for days at a time—but he put a hand up, cutting me off.

"I had a visit with a local healer while you slept this morning. She agrees with me that you need at least a week in bed."

My eyes narrowed, irritated that he would go to a healer after I specifically asked him not to. He must have caught the shift in my gaze, because he quickly added, "I didn't tell her anyone was here, just that I needed her advice for a family matter." I let out a short breath, releasing some of the fear that was building inside me. At least there was that small mercy.

"Anyway, she gave me a fresh salve to put on your cuts and bruises, and a tonic for any internal damage that may have been done. And she said at least a week in bed, even if your magic provides you with healing capabilities." He hesitated before stepping into the room, laying the bottles where the stack of books had been. His eyes caught mine as he straightened, righting his posture. I sucked in a shallow breath, noticing again the piercing hue of his rich brown eyes, catching in the sunlight streaming in through a nearby window.

I stumbled over my words, caught in the momentary reprise the sight of him had given me.

"Thank you—" I paused, suddenly realizing I couldn't recall his name. My cheeks flushed with heat as I searched the recesses of my mind for the details of the night before.

The corner of his lips tipped up as he watched me scrambling, reading my mind as he finished my statement for me:

"Bastian." He put his fist to his heart and bowed his head slightly, just as he had the night before in the woods. The gesture struck something in me, a piece of tradition and formality to let me know that he was a friend, not an enemy. Not something to be feared.

"Aermidh," I replied, awkwardly returning the gesture. "But my friends call me Aerie."

A playful smile danced across his lips. "So is that what we are, then? Friends?"

"Friends," I repeated, turning over the phrase again and again in my mind—testing it to see if it felt right. Finally, I sat back in my bed, flipping open one of the books from the stack. "We'll see."

He didn't respond as he backed out of the room. I peeked over the top of my book just enough to see him running a hand through his hair as he pulled the door shut behind him. But it was impossible to miss the chuckle that echoed off the walls as he retreated down the hallway and deeper into the estate.

CHAPTER 10
AERIE

Two weeks.

That's how long I stayed holed up in that wretched room. After the first week I was miserable. I found myself going stir-crazy, finding literally anything to pass the time. I finished the books Bastian had brought me within the first couple days, then reread them all again before giving up and resorting to counting the stones lining the hearth just to pass the time. Once my legs were feeling strong enough, I started forcing myself out of bed to walk laps around the small space until my bones ached and demanded I return to my rest. I was pushing to leave altogether, but Bastian somehow convinced me to stay another week, compromising with daily walks through the gardens and perhaps some visits to the library. The fact that his brother, Vander, hadn't shown his face again was a small mercy, lending me to feel slightly more comfortable with Bastian's request for me to stay. Though I reluctantly agreed, I knew the groaning of my joints and the lingering dizziness in my head were probably signs that my father's magic was still working its way out of my system. His magic should have subsided by now, replaced with the healing glow of my own. The fact that I could still feel it writhing through my veins worried me more than I wanted to admit.

I'd assumed the gardens would be a favorable, or at least an acceptable, reprise from the confines of my room—but upon my first day in the gardens I realized there were no workers keeping up with the demands of the estate. They were unruly, overrun with thorny weeds and decaying roots. What had assuredly once been a lush and lively garden was now dried and shriveled with months, if not years, of neglect.

Bastian had insisted on accompanying me on these walks, but he never spoke of the state of the gardens, never gave reason for why it'd been left to die and be overtaken by chaos—and I couldn't find the courage yet to ask. Still, It surprised me how easy it was to talk with Bastian, despite the differences between our people. I found myself longing for our walks, finding the conversation flowing between us oddly heartwarming. I found comfort in the stories he told of his youth, imagining the wide-eyed boy running through the trees and around the estate. It wasn't all that far off from the image of Bastian that I'd come to know over my short time here, that sense of wonderment and joy still hiding somewhere within those amber eyes.

By the end of the second week, my body was starting to feel much more like itself. The new marrings were starting to fade to match the old scars, and I could stand and walk without much pain, as long as I didn't push too hard. My mind, on the other hand, was just as much of a mess as it had been the day Bastian found me. Time had done nothing to heal those wounds; I felt the pain of losing my sisters every second of the day. It was a heavy cloud that hung around me, permeating my very being as I tried desperately to keep going.

Bastian seemed to notice that weight as we walked through the gardens, matching my silence. Noticing the slowing of my gait, he guided us to a small table surrounded by garden beds overrun with wildflowers. This corner of the garden was guarded. Quiet. I let my mind drift as I watched the nearby fluttering of insects between the array of blooms that had overtaken whatever had once been planted here.

He watched me carefully. I could feel the pregnant pause as he debated voicing whatever question was on his lips. "You haven't talked about what happened that night."

I looked away, trying not to let him see the tears pricking my eyes.

"You don't have to," he added quickly. "I've not brought it up because I wanted you to have time. To process, to heal, whatever you need. But it may be good for you to talk to someone about it."

"I don't have anyone to talk to," I replied solemnly. There was no one left in this world for me, no one who cared what happened or who'd want to help carry the burden of the scars I bore. I was my own keeper now.

"You have me," he offered, laying a hand on the table, his palm open to the sky as he waited for me to respond. I hesitated, unsure if I truly trusted him enough to be so vulnerable with him. My sisters were my family. A secret locked away in the depths of the Dark Woods for no one to find. Until someone did. Now, there was no reason not to trust Bastian, nothing left to lose if I were to open up to him.

"My sisters..." My voice shook as I tried to speak, the tears feeling almost impossible to hold back now. Without thinking, I placed my hand in Bastian's, the sheer size of his calloused palm engulfing mine. I felt him give me a reassuring squeeze as he encouraged me to keep going. "We lived together in that cottage. We all found each other during our darkest moments, members of society who had been cast away or lost. We made a home for each other, a chosen family. They taught me everything I know. Every good piece of me is because of them." I smiled as I felt the first tear fall down my cheek. "That is, until my father found me. I ran away from him, from his palace in hiding. He's one of the last fae kings, a cruel, evil testament to what the Old World was."

I stopped myself from sharing more, unable to explain the cruelty he'd shown me time and again throughout my years under his watch. As his captor. Instead, my mind went back to that night I came back to the cottage, a smoldering remnant of the joy it once was.

"He found me and took everything from me just to spite me for rejecting him. Rejecting his people. I never wanted any part of his plan—" I choked on a sob, trying to keep my composure from slipping, my free hand absent-mindedly clutching at my abdomen. The pain of my father's magic still lingered even now.

"It's okay to let yourself feel that here, Aerie. You don't have to spare your emotions for me." Bastian leaned forward, wrapping both his hands around mine. I nodded slightly, even if I didn't truly understand the sentiment. I'd already shared too much, let him see too far into my past. I tamped down on the emotions ravaging my mind, pushing the pain and the horror from my thoughts as I pulled my hand back and wiped my tears away.

"Anyway, that's when you found me. If you hadn't come when you did..." I trailed off, imagining the agony I'd still be in if he'd never found me there. If I would even be alive at all. I shook my head, turning my attention back to Bastian, who was still watching me intently.

"I think we've been out long enough," he said finally, standing up and holding out his arm. "It's time for some more rest."

I held back a groan but rose to meet him, grateful for someone to confide in. "Fine," I mumbled.

"And I'm glad," he said, as we made our way back into the estate.

"Glad?" I echoed.

He gave me a bittersweet smile, leaving me with no response all the way back to my room. He dropped my arm delicately, stepping out the door before turning back to call out over his shoulder with that same faint smile. "Glad that I found you."

Despite getting around the estate more than I had since arriving here, I found myself itching to *do* something. The walls of my room felt exceptionally suffocating today and no amount of trips to the library or garden could quiet the thoughts echoing throughout my mind. I was both grateful and embarrassed after my conversation with Bastian in the garden. The idea of being vulnerable with anyone again felt rather complicated. Careful not to run into Bastian, I snuck into the kitchen and rummaged around to see what he had in the way of acceptable ingredients before starting on a proper home-cooked meal. Much like the gardens, the kitchen wasn't being tended to by anyone other than Bastian, and his meals over the past two weeks had left much to be desired.

Within the hour, the kitchen was filled with the aromatic flavors of herb roasted potatoes and spiced meat. There hadn't been much to choose from in the root cellar, but a simple meal would suffice for tonight. I made a note to inquire about restocking the cellar. I moved about the kitchen with fluid ease as I cooked, prepping plates and cleaning dishes as I went. It was the most I'd felt like myself in the entire time I'd been here, and it was pleasing to see how quickly I fell into my own rhythm in such an unfamiliar space.

"What are you doing?" The words broke me from my trance, causing me to drop the utensils I was drying. My hand went to my heart as I tried to tame the rapid beating. Bastian was standing in the entryway to the kitchen, leaning against the wall and watching me from a distance, that familiar smirk plastered to his face. I shot him a look, throwing my towel at him before bending over to gather the utensils I'd dropped.

"You shouldn't sneak up on people like that," I scolded, reaching under the counter to fetch a wayward wooden spoon. "It isn't polite."

Bastian joined me, crouched on the floor, and collected the items he'd caused me to drop. "My apologies," he offered, though I could hear the sarcasm in his voice. I stood, setting my pile on the nearby counter, his joining mine a second later. "You were humming."

The statement gave me pause, feeling out of place in the small space between us. His eyes narrowed on me, his presence invading mine in a way that had me moving closer still.

"I was?" I hadn't realized. I used to hum as I worked at the cottage. The sound would drive my sisters crazy. I hadn't felt the desire to since coming here though, hadn't had a song worth singing since that dark day in the woods.

Bastian watched me a moment longer, reaching out to tuck a strand of hair behind my ear. His fingers lingered there for just a moment, grazing against the sensitive skin of my cheek. At some point, I supposed, he'd gotten over his fear of me, of my fae blood. Enough so that now he could be this close to me, touch me, and not feel the need to recoil or fight.

"You didn't answer my question," he whispered into the quiet space between us. My brows furrowed, not understanding what he meant. Forcing space between us, he backed away suddenly and gestured to the rest of the kitchen. "I asked what you were doing in here. You're supposed to be resting."

I steeled my expression, forcing a deep, subtle breath through my nose before trusting myself to speak. "Well after two weeks of whatever it was you call cooking, I figured it was time I show you what a proper meal tastes like."

I moved opposite him, gathering up the rest of the food and carrying it into the dining room, where I'd prepared the table. The room had been a pleasant surprise, full of light and warm decor. The table was large, much too large for just the two of us, but I couldn't stand the thought of eating another meal in my room or at the tiny table in the kitchen. Large windows lined the outer wall, flooding the deep mahogany table in the setting sunlight. I could practically see the kinds of dinners that must have been hosted here over the years, and it called for me to bring life back within its walls.

"Care to join me?" I called over my shoulder.

"Well, I'd hate to miss out on such an important lesson from you. And if it tastes half as good as it smells, you've already put me to shame." His voice was much closer than I anticipated, his brawny body towering right behind me as I moved around the table, setting dishes down and serving food to both of us. He slid into the seat at the head of the table and I chose one opposite him, if for no other reason than to force some distance between us after whatever moment we'd just shared in the kitchen.

He huffed out a laugh, grabbed his place setting and his food, and moved down the table to the chair directly next to me.

The food was delicious and I was grateful for my health returning so I could fumble about the kitchen long enough to cook it. I'd begun to wonder if I was suffering from starvation, the way my stomach protested at Bastian's sorry excuse for cooking. He ate even faster than I did, shoveling food in his mouth as if he'd never tasted anything as simple as meat and potatoes before.

"By the Fates, Aerie," Bastian said through a mouthful of food, "I can't remember the last time someone made me a true home-cooked meal, let alone something this divine." He stabbed the last of his potatoes with his fork before pushing his plate away and throwing his napkin on the table next to him.

"Yes, well, my sisters had many skills, cooking not being the least of them." I smiled, thinking of our times in the kitchen together, standing hip to hip as they taught me how to bake bread and chop vegetables—the most basic of tasks that I'd never been allowed to learn under my father's watch.

Bastian hummed, pulling my attention back to him.

"What?" I asked, mirroring the playful smile now dancing across his lips.

"You light up when you talk about them." His smile grew, bringing heat to my cheeks as I felt suddenly self-conscious about my own appearance.

"I do?" I asked almost absent-mindedly as I sat up a little straighter and fiddled with my fingers in my lap.

Bastian nodded, shifting in his seat to lean forward. "You did tonight in the kitchen as you served supper. You did just now, when you brought them up. And you did in the garden a few days ago when you first told me about them."

I dropped my gaze to my lap, unsure what to say. As much as it pained me to think of them, I couldn't help but find joy in knowing their light still shone within me.

"I'm sure it was hard for you to share their story." His voice dipped lower, softer, as if he understood how delicate a topic it was. How simply mentioning their existence took me right back to that night, back to the vile things my father did to me. Before my mind could drift into that darkness, he reached out, tenderly taking my hand in his. "It's so clear to see that they are a very important piece of you." His finger brushed over the back of my hand, sending tingles up my arm. "Thank you for trusting me with their story."

I nodded, pulling my gaze away from those piercing umber eyes. "Enough about me. What about you?"

"Me?" he asked, his tone questioning as his brows pinched together.

"You must have quite a story to share. The big bad chieftain in his estate all alone. For Fates' sake, you don't even have someone to cook and clean for you," I teased, pushing at his arm in an effort to lighten the mood. He laughed along with me, but it didn't quite reach his eyes.

"Trust me, there's no point in opening those wounds."

I cocked my head, viewing him for perhaps the first time through the eyes of loss and grief. I had to admit, in my short time here, I hadn't given much thought to the reasoning behind the quiet of the estate. We'd not talked much about his brother since that first night, and he never mentioned any other family. I wondered perhaps if he had sent everyone away to give me privacy as I recovered. But maybe there was more to it than that. Maybe we were more alike than I thought.

CHAPTER II
BASTIAN

I leaned back in my chair, trying to avoid those ice blue eyes. Not like the ice of a frigid, harsh winter—ice like the crisp freshness of a mountain spring, healing and refreshing. She'd had her harsher moments recovering in those early days, but even during her worst times, she was at most hesitant and scared. Never truly cold.

I knew if I stared too long into those eyes, they'd unravel me. Reveal each of my secrets and the pains of my past. Which is exactly why I was trying to find anywhere at all to look at besides her.

"This trust thing goes both ways." Something gleamed in her eye as she waited for me to reply. She wasn't playing fair. I was supposed to be here for *her*. To support her, to take care of her. Yet somehow, she had offered me as much healing in these past two weeks as I hoped I had to her. It had been so long since I'd had another soul to speak to within these walls. Someone to live life beside, even if that was a poor description for what we'd been doing. For the most part we'd been trying to avoid one another, give each other space as we navigated around the awkwardness of this new dynamic.

"I'm an open book," I lied. "What do you want to know?"

She rested her elbow on the table, leaning her head against her hand as she tapped her finger against her face in thought. "Did you send everyone on your estate away when you brought me home? Or is it always this… quiet?" She chose her last word carefully, a sort of thoughtfulness that I couldn't help but appreciate.

"It's been this… *quiet* for a long time." She waited patiently for me to explain. When I finally realized I wouldn't escape her questioning, I let out a resigned breath. "My parents died quite some time ago, leaving the estate to me and my brother. We were starting to get the hang of running an estate like this, not to mention the tribe, when…" I broke off, my voice faltering as I tried to mention Hazlenn's name. The familiar sting of loss echoed through my soul.

"Vander and I had a friend, a sister of sorts. Someone we grew up with who held a lot of importance in our lives. After Vander took over as chieftain, she went missing and it sort of… made everything crumble." I balled my hands into fists, trying to tame the storm of emotion inside me.

"You and this female… you were involved?" Her question was so innocent, so genuine, but it did nothing to stop the coarse laugh that broke from my throat.

"Me and Hazlenn? No, no it wasn't like that. She was like a sister to me." I paused, thinking back on the days when the three of us would run through the tribe's land, following the border as far as our parents would let us go, just to see if we could find our way back. "Now Vander, that's a different story. I always suspected his feelings were stronger. Something different was growing between them."

I swallowed around the lump in my throat, trying to get a grip on my grief ripping through me almost as strong as the day it all happened. "He was with her the day she was taken. I'm not sure what happened, but he... he didn't come back the same." A chill crept over my skin, and I ran a hand through my hair to shake off the feeling. "I took over as chieftain shortly after, and he took off into the Dark Woods to find her. Not much of the staff stuck around that long and any who had, I dismissed eventually. It felt odd having so many other people in here when none of my family remained in these halls."

I blinked as I noticed the warmth shifting along my arm, looking down. Aerie had moved closer and rested her hand against me.

"I'm so sorry that you've lost so much of your family, Bastian. It is a pain I'd wish on no one." Understanding, sympathy, and the familiar look of grief stared back at me in those bright blue eyes. I nodded, knowing now that she knew that pain all too well. She hesitated for a moment, the features of her face wrinkled in thought, before she moved closer. "I can take the pain away... if you'd like."

"What do you mean? I asked, inclining my chin towards her. With each passing second, her presence grew closer towards mine, the warmth of her touch trickling down my arm and through my body.

"My magic. It has the power to heal. Physical ailments, mental ones. It doesn't matter. I can ease the burden on your mind, make it hurt just a little less for the time being." She must have sensed my unease because she gave my arm a reassuring pat as she added, "It's the least I could do, as a thank you for all you've done to help me."

I gave her a tight nod—my jaw tightening, unsure what to expect.

I couldn't do anything but watch her as she moved with hypnotic grace, her magic beginning to weave through my body with disturbing ease. It was almost too difficult to care, feeling the peace and warmth that her touch brought me. Sunbeams danced across my skin, sinking deep and heating parts of me that had long gone cold. I closed my eyes and fell into the trance taking over me, suddenly no longer in the dining room but rather floating in the water of a babbling river. I could hear the melodic music of a bluejay just above, could feel the cool water run through my hair and between my toes. The smell of sweetgrass swirled around me and I let out a long, slow breath—relishing in the magic swimming through my body.

Too soon, the vision drifted away like a distant dream just beyond my reach. I blinked my eyes open as the weight returned to my body. I recognized the table before me, the dining room where I'd grown up eating meals with my family. But in the distance, somewhere deep within my soul, I could still hear the trickling of river water over stones, could still feel the warmth of the sun in my veins.

"Thank you," I breathed, spellbound. She returned a gentle smile back. "Is it possible for you to use your magic on yourself?" I asked, forcing myself to retreat just the slightest amount from the closeness of her body. She froze at my question, a mask of guarded indifference sliding into place.

"It is," she answered coolly.

"But you haven't." It wasn't a question. I knew the fae were fast healers, that the tribes inherited that lovely little skill from their fae forefathers, but even with that ability she'd been surprisingly slow to heal, both mentally and physically. I wondered how much of that was intentional, how much she was keeping her magic at bay to prolong the hurt she was feeling. I bristled at the thought of the nightmares she must have experienced at the hand of her supposed father. My blood boiled to know a male could be so cruel to their own blood, to their own daughter.

Aerie didn't reply right away. I could see each part of her mind turning over what I'd said, trying to come up with an appropriate response. Her hand still rested on my forearm, but the warmth of her touch was retreating, barely recognizable anymore. The more it receded the more I chased after it, silently screaming for more of it.

"I suppose I'm not ready to let go of the pain yet," she finally answered. Her honesty surprised me. I'd expected her to remain guarded, but the truth of her answer rang deep within me. I slowly laid my hand across hers, pausing only long enough to catch her gaze before giving her a reassuring squeeze.

"Maybe we can learn how together."

I might have had the willpower to resist her at supper, but as I tossed and turned in bed all night I realized that I was fighting a losing battle. This mysterious little fae from the depths of the Dark Woods had captured more than just my eye. Her touch was a siren song I longed to hear more of. Visions of her alabaster skin beneath my finger tips, between my teeth, haunted my dreams that night and forced me to eventually abandon my bed and stalk the halls of the empty estate. So many haunting memories were flooding my mind tonight, and mixed with the idea of *her*—it was a recipe for unrest.

Before long I found myself making my way out the door and into the early morning dawn. Calling to the primal form within me, I allowed my wolven features to slip into place. Muscles stretched and shifted as my stride altered. My vision narrowed, sharpening details far ahead as I made a break for the nearby woods. I didn't often like to use my wolven form, especially now as chieftain. Not all in the earth tribe were shifters, and while it was truly an honorable power to hold, I would have been naive to not realize how uncomfortable it made those who didn't possess the ability. I knew as leader of the tribe it would be better for my people to see me as a levelheaded, strong leader. Not a wild animal incapable of controlling his impulses.

Now though... now I wasn't sure which I related to more. The feel of the grass beneath my paws, the natural instinct of my senses now heightened in my wolven form, the wind rustling my fur as I ran—they were all things that felt like second nature to me, things that I forgot how much I loved until moments like this. There were so many impulses vibrating through my body, so many instincts fighting for *her*, begging me to act on them without a second thought. But she was a hurting female under my care. I'd promised she'd be safe here and I wasn't about to take advantage of her vulnerability and trust simply because I hadn't been able to get her out of my mind.

The sun had risen high into the morning sky by the time I made my way back through the halls and into my bedroom. Shifting back into my mortal form, I took a quick bath and rummaged through my wardrobe long enough to find some half decent clothing for the day. On top of maintaining the estate and attending to tribe matters, I was also running behind on laundry it would seem.

Aerie was already in the kitchen as I made my way there, cooking what smelled like a delicious breakfast of porridge and coffee. I hummed in approval as I poured myself a large mug of the beautiful dark liquid.

"I could get used to this," I teased as I drank deeply from the overfull mug. "Breakfast *and* coffee ready and waiting for me as soon as I wake up? I couldn't imagine a more beautiful thing." That was a lie. I *could* imagine, but I didn't have to. She was standing right in front of me smirking with a sarcastic smile as I sipped from my mug once more.

"Yes, well, I will expect you to start stepping in at some point. What do you expect to do once I'm gone if you just rely on me to do everything for you while I'm still here?"

I faked a laugh, the idea of her leaving at some point sobering the playful edge in my voice.

"And don't lie to me, you've been up for hours. I saw you stalking around the estate this morning."

I coughed, choking on the sip I'd just taken. "You... saw me? This morning?"

"Oh, yes. It was kind of hard to miss the oversized wolf doing laps around the house just outside my window." She turned back to the cast iron stove and continued stirring the porridge.

"And what did you think when you saw the oversized wolf doing laps just outside your window?" I half mumbled into my mug as I waited in rigid hesitation for her response.

She paused, still with her back to me as she thought it over for a minute. "Not bad." She ladled the creamy porridge into a bowl, turning to set it down in front of me at the large kitchen counter where I was drinking my coffee. Leaning against the counter, she rested her head on her hand as she met my gaze with a wicked smile. "For a dog."

I felt my own smile grow as I watched that mischievous sense of humor dance in her eyes. I picked up a spoonful of my breakfast, relishing in the warm comfort of the simple meal. Swallowing my bite, I pointed my spoon at her. "Keep making food like this and maybe I'll let you get away with making comments like that. Maybe."

She threw her head back and laughed, the sound bringing pure joy to my soul. She moved through the kitchen, her laughter echoing all around us, as she took the pot off the fire and set it beside us on the counter.

"Oh, by the way," she said as she grabbed a scrap of parchment and set it down beside me. "I made a list of things you need to restock on, plus a few extras if you don't mind." She tapped the paper carefully before grabbing the coffee and refilling both our mugs.

I grabbed the list, looking over the items. "Shouldn't be a problem. I can make a trip into the nearby town today and get everything." Though, I didn't recognize everything on the list. "What are these?" I asked, pushing the list back towards her and tapping the unfamiliar names.

Aerie's face drained of color. She turned her attention back to her bowl, mumbling an answer in between spoonfuls of her porridge.

"What was that?" I asked.

She sighed, rubbing her thumb and forefinger on her forehead as she set her spoon down and looked up at me. "It's ingredients for a spell."

"A spell?" I repeated, a little shocked by the response. The fae, from what I'd heard, weren't typically ones for witchcraft.

Aerie sighed, leaning back and running her hands over her crossed arms as she glanced around the kitchen nervously. "Look, I'll understand it if you don't want me here after today, but I need those ingredients and—"

"Why would I want you to leave? Because you're mixing a spell?"

Aerie scoffed, leveling her gaze at me. "I'm not that naive, Bastian. I know the negative connotation that witchcraft holds. Why do you think my sisters and I lived so deep within the Dark Woods?"

"Aerie," I chided, sitting back and fixing her with a resolute look. "I don't know what else I can do to make you feel safe here, but it's going to take a lot more than a little witchcraft to force you out of this estate. Besides, I like to think the earth tribe is more progressive than holding onto those Old World hateful biases and stereotypes."

I could tell by the way she stilled that my words shocked her. "I can't speak for everyone in my tribe, but I, as well as many others here, uphold witchcraft with the same respect and reverence as any other skill set amongst our people."

Tears brimmed in her eyes as she sat and stared at me.

If anything, finding out that she practiced witchcraft made me respect and admire her even more. It wasn't an easy skill to master and if she knew the spell well enough to recite ingredients from memory, I supposed she was rather practiced in her craft. It struck me that complete and total acceptance was perhaps not something she'd ever experienced before, or at least experienced often enough. I wanted to reach out to her, to wrap her in my embrace and whisper away every self-loathing and doubtful thought she had.

Instead, I took one more sip of coffee, grabbed the list, and pushed off the chair. "I'll head into town this morning, I have some business to attend to anyway."

She blinked away the tears threatening to spill over her eyes as she shook her head free of whatever thoughts were circling there.

"Anything else you can think of that you may need?" I moved to the side door, grabbing my cloak off the hook and fastening it over my shoulders.

"Um…" She followed me to the door, abandoning her half eaten breakfast, still sitting on the table. "Perhaps some seeds for the garden? I was thinking I could maybe start tending to it. You know, just while I'm here. I could get it back in a passable condition for you before I leave."

I tried to stifle the urge to grit my teeth at the mention of her leaving. Two comments about it in one morning were more of a reminder than I cared for. But I nodded anyway, imagining how much I'd love to see her out in the garden. It used to be my mother's place of reprieve.

"I'll add it to the list." My voice was rougher than I'd meant for it to be as I replied to her, failing to bite back the irritation that had worked its way through my body at the thought of her leaving. I pushed through the door without looking back, not trusting myself to not beg her to stay if I lingered a moment longer in that kitchen.

CHAPTER 12
AERIE

Days passed as I tried to focus on my healing and not on the fact that I was starting to get too comfortable here. I knew it was a dangerous thing, getting used to being in this house, with that male. This wasn't my place, my home. And I needed to remember that. I wasn't sure how much longer he'd allow me to stay in this place. My body had all but returned to normal; my wounds had long since faded, leaving tender pink flesh in their stead. The bottles Bastian had gotten from the healer seemed to speed up my healing process. I should have been grateful. But that paired with how he left me in the kitchen the other day only had me convinced he was ready to be rid of me.

But truthfully, it didn't matter if that was what he truly wanted or not. I knew deep down that I'd never make it in a place like this either way. The tribe would never accept a fae member; the way Bastian's brother had reacted to my being here was proof enough for that. And after everything I'd done at my father's hand, I couldn't say I disagreed. It would be better for me out there on my own, once I figured out how to rid myself of my father's hold, once and for all.

I spread the assortment of ingredients Bastian had acquired for me out across the surface of my bed—several crystals of varying hues, pouches of dried herbs and animal bones—and took careful count that everything I'd need was there. I'd been surprised to find that he'd had a couple things on hand already. I pulled those out from beneath my bed and added them to the collection.

I took a deep breath, my nerves rattled beyond belief as I tried to remember everything Flora had taught me. I hadn't practiced any form of witchcraft since I'd lost them. Doing it now, in a room that wasn't even mine and without my sisters by my side, felt wrong. I closed my eyes and pictured them, memories of us together and happy flashing through my mind. It steadied my hands as I picked up the first ingredient and dumped it into the bowl.

I spoke in an ancient language as I added more and more of the herbs and oddities sitting around me, taking care that I added them in the right order. Not too much of one thing, just enough of another. It came as easy as breathing. Within a matter of minutes, all of the ingredients were added and all that was left was the last step—my blood. My head snapped up from the bowl, suddenly overwhelmed with the presence of my sisters. The same peace that so often accompanied me on our nights by the fire, or days cooking in the kitchen and tending to the garden, washed over me, flooding my body with a kind of strength and courage that was unmistakably theirs. Whimpering, I took them in—their spirits, their warmth, their love.

They were here. They were always here. I understood now that I had to carry on their stories, that using what they taught me would only ever honor them. And that they'd always be with me for the difficult moments like this. My chin trembled as I bit back tears. My gaze fell to the bowl before me, my hands moving of their own accord as something otherworldly—the strength of my sisters—spurred me to keep going.

I slipped a knife from its leather sheath on the bed and placed my hand over the bowl, letting the cool metal slice into the tender skin of my palm. My blood dripped onto the mixture in the bowl, its metallic scent invading my nose. I squeezed my fist, encouraging more to flow, covering the herbs in a crimson bath. The spell took hold, magic thrumming through my body in earnest search.

I cried out in pain as it found its target, writhing and fighting with the remnants of my father's magic inside me. I fell back on the bed in agony, knocking over the bowl of herbs and throwing the contents across the room. The subtle presence of my sisters' peace dulled with the movement, my mind and spirit cast into an endless, hopeless sort of despair. I clutched at my body, fingernails digging at my skin. I could feel the spell dying within me. The power of my father's magic was too strong, the mark it had left within me too dark.

"No, no, no." My voice sounded raw as I begged for the spell to keep going, to fight harder. I backed it with my own fae magic in a desperate attempt to help it succeed. But it was no use. The magic faded as I felt my father's power settle back into place. I could almost hear the wicked pitch of his laughter in my mind at such a futile attempt to be rid of him. Whatever he'd done to me, there was no repairing it.

I sat up, breath heavy and covered in a cold sweat as I tried to wrap my mind around what this meant. I let out a rageful scream as I grabbed at my hair and buried my face in my hands. Even now, he still had a hold on me, still controlled my life and my future. I would never escape him.

That single thought had me burrowing down a dark path I knew I'd never recover from.

Hot, angry tears spilled down my face as I pushed off my bed and made towards the door. I needed fresh air, I needed the grass beneath my bare feet, I needed anything but being stuck in this stifling room with the remnants of the herbs and my blood spilled across the floor as a stark reminder for how much of a failure I was.

Ripping the door open, I stumbled backwards in shock to find Bastian standing there with a raised fist, like he'd been about to knock.

"What in the Depths are you doing, Aerie?" he asked, looking around the room. He grabbed me by the shoulders. "Are you okay?"

I clutched my hand to my chest as I tried to steady my racing heart, hastily wiping my face with the other hand, trying to hide the tears that were still falling.

"Aerie, what's wrong?" His eyes fell to the wound at my hand, the blood most likely smeared across my chest where I held it.

I brushed him away, trying to push past him out into the hall-way. His large frame was too strong though and he easily blocked my path, planting me in front of him and refusing to let me go. Understanding settled across his features as his eyes landed on the mess of herbs on the floor.

"What was the spell for, Aerie?"

"Nothing," I lied. "Just a simple healing spell."

"Are you still hurt?" His concern was etched across his face, woven through his words. I didn't have the strength to tell him the truth, to admit what the spell's failure confirmed.

"No, I was just trying to brush up on my spellwork. It's been weeks since I've been able to practice." I couldn't meet his gaze, my arms wrapped around myself as I kept my eyes carefully trained on the floor. But Bastian didn't buy my lies.

"Aermidh." It was the first time he'd used my full name. I didn't know how he'd even remembered it, as I'd only told him it once, when I'd first introduced myself. I sucked in a stunned breath as he hooked his finger around my chin and raised my head to meet his gaze. All the air left the room as I stared into his deep brown eyes, swirling with honeyed amber.

"What was the spell for?" he asked again, gentler, in a way that had me melting beneath his touch.

I took a deep, trembling breath before I found the nerve to answer. "When my father attacked me, he pierced me with his magic. Mentioned something about not letting my power pass on. I needed to know what he meant, needed to see how much damage his magic caused—is still causing—inside me."

"It's still there?" he asked quickly, taking a step back to look me over. He was already on the defensive, ready to strike down the threat. Like there was anything he could do against this power.

I nodded slowly. "All my life, his plan for me was to produce an heir for his people. He spent so much time strengthening my power, embedding it with more magic in an effort to make me the most powerful fae our kind had ever seen. All for the sake of passing that power along to an heir someday, someone that would lead our revolution and retain our place in the world."

I tried to stifle a whimper as I came to the crux of the issue, what the spell confirmed and the truth that was screaming through my entire body. "He took that ability away. Now that I've *defiled* myself, he won't touch me. But he made sure that the power he's worked so hard to cultivate will never be passed down through my bloodline." I took a deep breath, letting the last of my tears fall before stating the final truth: "Because there will be no future bloodline for me."

Bastian didn't speak. There were no words that would make this better, no words that would make what my father did to me okay. The absolute betrayal and assault of his actions, changing my body and my future without my consent. Causing me pain on every level and making sure I'd never be able to escape his grasp. Bastian knew it just as much as I did. He pulled me into his embrace, wrapped me in the warmth of his arms and let me cry.

"I'm so sorry, Aerie," he whispered into my hair as he ran his hand through the strands. The low rumble in his chest turned darker, something closer to growling. "I vow to you, I will find him. And I will kill him for what he's done to you."

I pulled back, shocked by his promise. "This isn't your battle."

Bastian just shook his head, refusing to let it go. "It won't be today, maybe not even this year. I will put your safety above everything else, and that means giving you time to move on from this. But what he's done to you cannot go unpunished. And as long as he walks this earth, he remains a threat to you." He pulled my face into his hands, leveling our gazes. "Let me do this for you, Aerie."

I just stared in awe of the male before me, a stranger in the night who turned out to be one of the purest beings. I couldn't let him get involved in this mess of fae wrath and war. He was too good for them. He'd get torn to shreds in an instant. But I could see there was no arguing with him in this moment. In time, he'd forget his vow—I was sure of it. I'd move on and find a new life and be nothing but a faint memory in his mind. Hopefully one he'd look back on with fondness, but nothing more. It could be nothing more.

"Now," he said, finally letting me go and backing away. Only our hands remained in each other's grasp as he pulled me through the doorway. "I have something to show you. If you're feeling up for it. It may help you feel better."

I forced a smile, nodding my head slightly. I was desperate to get away from this room, away from the haunting feeling of my father and all he'd done to ruin me. Bastian offered me a small smile before turning and leading me through the hall and into the kitchen. On the table sat a crate of tools and supplies. He gestured for me to take it, so I stepped up to the wooden box and looked through the contents.

Gardening tools, supplies of the highest quality. I recognized common herbs for practicing witchcraft, as well as seeds of more extravagant plants—some I hadn't even heard of before. I didn't know how he'd known which ones to buy, but somehow he'd supplied me with a whole assortment to build the most perfect garden.

"Bastian," I whispered, running my fingers over the soft linen of a sage green smock he'd picked out for me. I was unable to find quite the right words to express my gratitude towards him.

"That's not all," he said. He was almost bouncing as he led me out the door and towards the overgrown, unruly gardens. In their place, I found empty tilled land ready and waiting to be sown.

I was stunned beyond words. It was the nicest gift I'd ever received. And it made it hurt even more that I knew I wouldn't be able to stay here, that this was just a stepping stone to whatever was next in my journey. I'd never be able to find a place here, a fae amongst the tribes. No matter the pain that thought brought me, I pushed it away. Stifled its sting until it was shoved into the recesses of my mind and just a mere echo. I wouldn't let it ruin this moment.

I turned to the side, where pieces of wood lay in the grass next to the garden, outlined in a large rectangular shape.

"What is that for?" I asked, stepping towards the odd sight.

Bastian grabbed my hand, pulling my attention back towards him. "I have big plans for that area over there, but it's a surprise.

You're not allowed to know yet. I just needed to make sure it would fit with the gardens here."

"What is it?" I pressed, tilting my head as I watched the mischievous wrinkles in his smile.

"You'll see," he said, beaming.

CHAPTER 13
BASTIAN

I threw back the last of the contents in my glass, letting the warm spirits burn all the way down my throat. Today had been taxing, as every day recently had been. Vander had yet to return since that first day I'd brought Aerie to the estate. Fates knew where he was, and if he didn't care enough to tell me what the fuck he was doing these days then I didn't care enough to worry.

Aerie was another issue entirely. From what I could tell, she'd healed up rather quickly from what happened to her. But I knew it was still weighing heavily on her. She'd shared bits and pieces of the story, but I gathered there was still a lot I didn't understand. Regardless of whatever she wasn't telling me, it had been nice having her here. It had gotten rather lonely since my parents' passing, even more so after we lost Hazlenn—when I lost Vander.

I poured myself another full glass of sunbeam whiskey and drained it down to the dregs. I feared our time together was limited. Even after I'd given her the garden, I could tell she still planned to leave. I was hoping that by offering her a place here, showing her that her skills were needed amongst the estate, would perhaps convince her to stay. But I feared she'd grow tired of this mundane life. This estate was a sorry excuse for a home, and the last thing I wanted to do was pile on to the trauma she was already trying to work through.

But seeing her in the garden these past few days, just like my mother used to do... it was like watching the Divine herself, planting and creating life. It was absolute bliss. I couldn't help but notice the way her spirit had lifted some, her head held a bit higher, a lighter air in her step. I laughed to myself, realizing just how thoroughly fucked I was by this female. She had a stronghold on my soul and she didn't even know it.

A noise outside the window caught my attention as I reached to fill a third glass. I cursed under my breath as I watched Aerie slip through the night and head for the trees. What the fuck was she thinking going out into the Dark Woods by herself? And at night, no less? Countless nightmares lurked in there—my brother, for one. I peered up at the bright night sky, catching sight of the full moon, and suddenly realized it had been a whole month she'd been staying with me.

I grumbled to myself as I pushed off the sofa and made for my axes. The full moon only meant that the woods would be more active, more erratic with threats and danger. I had to go after her. I wouldn't let her fall into harm's way again while under my care.

I crept quickly across the estate grounds and into the tree line, tracking her scent—rose and something spiced like patchouli—as I watched for movement within the trees. Just ahead I could make out her light hair bobbing through the dark shadows of the trees.

Where was she going?

I let out an irritated huff as I made my way through the woods after her. After what felt like an eternity of tracking and trailing her, Aerie finally came to a stop in a small clearing not far from the spot I'd originally found her. About fifty paces back I almost gave up and went home, assuming she had just decided to make a run for it. That perhaps our time was finally up. The thought made my stomach drop though, and my feet refused to listen to my head as I argued that we needed to let her go. If she didn't want to be here, then I couldn't make her stay.

But visions of the day I found her, buried in that burning cottage and left for dead flashed through my mind. It didn't matter if she was fae, if she didn't belong amongst the tribes, or if she thought she didn't deserve my attention. I could never damn her to that kind of torment. Just like I wouldn't leave her out here tonight, alone and defenseless to whatever creatures lurked in the shadows. Or worse, to be found by that vile fae king himself.

I watched from the tree line as she moved around the clearing. At first she did nothing but look around, as if she was lost within her mind entirely. She took in the scene of the trees, the grass, the clouds covering the moon, and the sound of insects drifting through the night's air. But when the clouds cleared and the moonbeams hit the small clearing, she laid down the blanket she had wrapped around her shoulders and broke into a series of motions beneath the moonlight. The gray fabric of her flowing skirts twirled around her as she spun, the somber color coming to life beneath the moonlight. She danced to a music only she could hear, her body moving freely and untamed as the silver light bounced off her alabaster skin.

It was pure ecstasy watching her like this. The most unabashed version of her I'd seen yet. Something told me this, this right here, was who she truly was. Without all of the pain, without the grief and loss and haunting memories of her past. Tonight she was just Aerie, dancing beneath the moon and amongst the trees, her own small version of nature's perfection.

She finally collapsed on the blanket, chest heaving as she tried to catch her breath. She threw her head back and laughed, the most joyous sound in the world, and I leaned in to get a better look.

A twig snapped beneath my boot. I cringed at the ferocity of the sound that I was sure gave me away.

"You can come out, you know," she called through the clearing, her back turned to me. "There's no use acting like I haven't known you were following me this whole time."

I let loose a shallow breath as I emerged from the trees and made my way to the blanket, taking a seat beside her. I shrugged off my cloak and offered it to her—noticing the way the top of her dress kept slipping down her arms—but she shook her head, leaning on the heels of her palms and letting her head fall back to extend her exposed shoulders to the moon.

"I don't want to miss a minute of this moonlight." She acted as if she was bathing in the sun, soaking up its warmth. The silken fabric of her sleeping gown pulled against her chest and drew me in within an instant. Seeing the thinness of the material hiding practically nothing in the moonlight, I quickly averted my gaze, trying to cling to my last shred of dignity tonight.

"Aren't you going to ask me what I'm doing out here?" She peeked open an eye as she waited for me to reply.

I cleared my throat, trying to formulate words well enough to answer. "Aerie, with you I've learned it's best to just not ask questions. Best to just sit back and watch you in your element."

She smiled at that, opening both eyes to watch me watch her. Her smile fell though, as she lay back fully and rested on the forest floor, one arm behind her head and motioning me to join her.

I set my cloak to the side, unharnessing my axes and placing them with the cloak before lying down beside her.

"Boots too, Chieftain." She winked at me as I looked at her in disbelief.

"Really?" I scoffed, assuming she was trying to mess with me.

"Really," she answered in earnest. "This is sacred ground tonight. You either tread on it with your bare skin or you don't touch it at all." I heard the way her tone dropped, the serious edge to her words, so I obeyed without argument, pulling my boots off and settling back down beside her. We lay there for some time, just admiring the beauty of the moon, watching how the clouds wove themselves around its glow.

"This was where my sisters and I would go every full moon." she said at last. My heart dropped, understanding at last why this ground was sacred to her. "We'd dance beneath the moonlight, eat together, offer ourselves to the moon and whatever she had in store for us, our futures, our life threads." She paused, taking a deep breath like there was more she wanted to share, but couldn't find the words.

"This was one of the last places I was with them. Before—" Her words cut off, but I didn't need her to explain. "With it being the first full moon since losing them, it only felt right to come back here."

I reached beside me to find her free hand and took it in mine as a silent promise to stay with her. Not just for tonight. For as long as she'd let me.

CHAPTER 14
AERIE

Bastian's hand felt like a tangible hope within my own. I didn't want to admit how much I felt myself falling for him. I wanted this, wanted *him*. But it felt like a reality that I didn't deserve. Even moreso, it felt like one that I'd never have. He was a tribal chieftain. I was a runaway fae with more scars than I could count. I had no business being here, finding a place for myself by his side, beneath his touch.

Even if it was a fool's hope, nothing that I'd ever be able to attain for myself, it didn't stop me from turning towards him—did nothing to keep me from running a hand through his chestnut hair as he leaned into my touch.

Even if we couldn't have a life together, we at least had tonight. It was a delusional thought, something that I had no business think-ing—let alone acting on. But as Bastian's eyes locked on mine, he saw every bit of intent and desire in my hooded gaze. He pushed off the ground to turn towards me, enveloping me with his warmth as he leaned in. Then paused, waiting for me to tell him this is what I truly wanted. An entire conversation passed between us with nothing more than piercing gazes.

Slowly, I nodded, hoping he understood just how much I needed this. He reached a hand to my head, tucking a strand of hair behind my ear and outlining the shape before trailing his calloused thumb down my jawline and to my lips. The rough feel of his skin against mine brought gooseflesh to the surface, had me leaning in desperate for more. He wrapped his hand around the back of my neck, finally pulling me into him. His lips felt warm and inviting against mine, pulling me under entirely as I parted to let his tongue claim me.

He tasted rich and smoky, some sort of spirits still lingering on his breath from the evening. I chased the taste, wanting more and more of it until I was intoxicated off the sheer remnant of it on his lips. He slid his hand down my front, the silk of my sleeping gown beneath his fingers, clutching the fabric in his fist as he deepened the kiss.

He groaned into my mouth as I arched my back towards him, begging for him to touch me—craving the feel of his kind fingers against my skin. He pulled me up, raising my hands above my head as he lifted my gown off. The chill of the night's air had my nipples pebbling instantly and a new wave of desire washed over me as I watched how Bastian took notice. He slid his tunic over his head in one swift motion, grabbing me in a blur of movement and pushing me back against the ground. He looked down on me with that same annoying smirk across his face as he trailed his fingers down my body, weaving over the dips and curves and enjoying every moment of it.

I gasped as his hands trailed lower, his grip tightening around my thigh as he nudged me to part for him. Nerves took hold as I tried to clear my mind from the fog of desire long enough to fathom the words I was trying to speak.

"Bastian, I—" My words we cut off as he leaned forward, kissing delicately at my chest until he found the peak of my breast and sucked it between his teeth. I shrieked, shocked by the motion. Even more shocked at how much I wanted him to do it again.

"What were you saying?" he asked with a wicked smile on his face.

I tried to regain my composure, swallowing hard as I looked at the chiseled, wide planes of his bare chest.

"I've never—" I started again, failing for a second time to voice the fear racing through my mind alongside the desire for him.

Understanding dawned on him, his eyes going wide as he gripped my hip in an effort to stop himself from moving further.

"Never?" he repeated.

I shook my head, hoping I hadn't just pushed him away with my untimely confession.

"My father refused to let the opportunity arise, insisted on keeping me pure for the right moment. And after I ran away, well, I was mostly focused on trying to remain hidden from him." I pulled my eyes away, suddenly feeling shameful.

Bastian took a deep breath, letting his head fall to my chest as he processed what I'd just admitted. It was only a moment's reprieve until he was back to trailing kisses across my chest, making his way back to my lips.

"Then I'll make sure to be gentle," he whispered against the side of my face, kissing his way to my ear. "For now." He nipped playfully at the tender flesh and I stifled a shriek. The sound died on my tongue, replaced with the sound of laughter as I rested my head in the curve of his neck.

He kissed and licked as I breathed heavily against his skin, begging for every touch. I was so lost in the moment that I hadn't even realized his fingers had made their way back between my thighs, and I gasped as I felt him begin stroking there. My head fell back as he worked me over, slipping a finger inside me, then another.

I was lost to this world, at the mercy of this male, *my male*. At least for tonight. This was everything I could have ever hoped for and I refused to think about the reality that I wouldn't have him for long. I cried out in pure pleasure as he continued his movement, my back arching off the ground and pushing against his punishing hand. I wanted more. I wanted to feel him fully and give him as much pleasure as he was giving me.

"Bastian," I pleaded, finding his gaze steadily trained on my face when I opened my eyes. "I want... more," I whispered into the heated space between us. "I want to feel all of you."

His eyes darkened as his hand stilled. My hips pushed against him in protest, pulling a smirk from his lips. "Yes, ma'am."

Within an instant he was gone, the lack of his presence leaving me cold and needy. He rolled back on his knees, undoing the fastenings on his pants and shoving them down to let his length spring free. My eyes widened, entirely unsure how I'd ever be able to take him, but knowing that would do nothing to deter me from trying. He centered himself over me, lowering till we were chest to chest, lips to lips.

"I'm going to go slow, okay? If it hurts too much, just tell me to stop and I will."

I nodded, sucking in a breath in preparation to feel him. His lips crashed onto mine again as he knocked my legs apart to make room for him—positioning himself at my entrance with a sweet and slow kind of tenderness. He deepened his kiss with every inch he sank into me. Every grimace of pain across my face he chased away with a reward of pleasure. He sucked at the tender flesh on my neck, kissed at each of my breasts and ran the pad of his thumb over their peaks. It was the best type of pain, the kind that I wanted to chase forever.

He pulled his face away, rocking slowly inside of me as I adjusted to the feel of him. Once he saw the pain in my face fade away, replaced only with desperate need, he guided my arms to his neck. "Hold on," he whispered, making sure I did as I was told before flipping us around so that I was on top of him.

I looked down at him, a question on the tip of my tongue, but it was gone as I took in the sight of him beneath me. His rugged skin was practically glowing, each chiseled crevice and hard line illuminated under the moon.

"I wanted to see you in the moonlight," he explained, letting his hands glide over my bare skin, taking notice of each and every scar now on full display for him to see. I closed my eyes, waiting for him to comment on them, for his desire to turn to disgust or rage as he took them in.

"You are so beautiful," his words vibrated through the night air.

I shook my head. "I'm not," I argued. I knew the marks that covered my skin, of the past they signified. "Bastian, there's so much you don't know, things I've done—" He held a finger up to my lips.

"You. Are. So. Beautiful," he repeated, letting the words wash over me in a cleansing wave of acceptance. "Your body, your spirit, it is all so beautiful, Aerie. And I know you don't believe me. But don't do me the disservice of arguing. Just hear it, and let me show you how much I believe it for you."

I looked down at him, at this male who had found me damaged and discarded. I didn't know what cruel twist of fate had caused him to show me kindness, but I was falling for it—for him—even though I knew I could never have a place beside him.

I swallowed back my fear, nodding at last in agreement to what he had asked of me—and I let him show me exactly how much he believed it.

His body guided mine, our naked forms coming to life in the moonlight. Silver beams swirled over our skin as we gave way to the primal need taking over us. It was a dance of desire. His fingers dug into my bare skin, ran up the length of my spine, laced through my hair. He was everywhere around me and within me all at once.

Time itself felt as if it stood still, just to preserve this moment between us.

Our dance became more frantic, frenzied, as I tipped my head back to the moon and lost myself entirely in the pleasure consuming my body. I cried out, overcome by the fever pitch. I was answered only by the low, feral growl of his own release, fingers digging into my hips as he held me against him.

Silence filled the clearing—the only sound, our ragged breathing as I buried myself against Bastian's chest. He said nothing to me as we tried to catch our breath. He just shifted me to the crook of his arm, wrapping me in his embrace and stroking my hair softly as we watched the sky above. I didn't need him to speak, didn't need him to confirm that he felt what I did just now. It was more than just sex, more than just lust or attraction. It was as if here, beneath the moon and the stars above, our souls were twining together, woven in a complicated tapestry made of need and grief and moonlight.

CHAPTER 15
BASTIAN

I couldn't sleep no matter how hard I tried. Aerie's skin was smooth as silk beneath my fingers as I brushed them over her arm. She was curled against my side, secure in my arms as we lay in my bed back at the estate. Tonight had been perfect. Pure magic. But it made me fear for what would come next. I could tell Aerie was restless here, looking for a way out and a new journey to embark on. Now that I had her, I couldn't fathom letting her go.

I breathed in her scent as she wrapped an arm around me in her sleep. I'd walked her back here after our time in the Dark Woods, after everything she'd revealed to me beneath the moonlight. I could sense those thoughts of worry and doubt starting to creep back in as we made our way back home, so I hadn't let her go back to her own room. I led her here, pinned her against my door, and planted kisses in a determined path till I'd landed at the very center of her desire, taking her again and again until we both collapsed and she drifted into a deep sleep.

There was so much I'd wanted to say tonight, so many plans I'd already constructed in my mind that I wanted to share with her, ask her. But now was not the time for that and I'd forced myself to pull back, letting her have the time to process this very large step. I smiled to myself in the darkness of the bedroom, imagining how many more ways I'd like to repeat that step with her.

A loud banging sounded from somewhere inside the estate and I jumped out of bed in an instant, trying to move with as much grace as I could muster in order not to wake Aerie. My hackles were raised, my senses on high alert to determine the source of the ruckus. I slipped on my pants and grabbed one of the axes leaning against the wall. I moved silently through the hall, scanning the rest of the rooms and following the sound of the continuous cacophony.

"Bastian!" My brother's voice boomed through the estate, calling for me. I let loose a breath of relief, thankful it was only him and not Aerie's father coming to finish what he'd started. I set my axe against the wall as I quickened my step into the sitting room.

My relief was short lived as I realized what he held in his hands, the reasoning behind the urgency in his tone.

"Is that—" My voice faltered as my steps carried me to my brother. Horror overtook me, rage and nausea fighting to take me down.

"Mirren." Vander finished my question for me. She was barely recognizable, covered in so much blood that I prayed to the Fates it wasn't her own. Her tiny, fragile fawn-like body dangled between Vander's arms.

"Is she..." I couldn't find the strength to say the last word.

Vander shook his head fervently. "No, I saved her before it could get to that. There was an attack along the border. One of Kahlis' creatures got through and practically took out the entire village nearby."

The village we placed Mirren in when her brothers went off on assignment because there was no one else to take care of her. That must have been six years ago. She'd been little more than an infant, but she'd grown so much since then. And now here she was, covered in blood and at the center of even more violence and destruction. She deserved so much better. I should have kept her here, made sure she was safe. Even if I was in no condition to raise a child.

"How the fuck did this happen?" I rushed to Vander, taking the poor girl from him and laying her on the sofa, using the linen he had wrapped around her in a crude attempt to clean off her face.

Before Vander could answer, Aerie emerged from the hall, wrapped in nothing more than a bedsheet. Her eyes went wide as she recognized Vander's presence. She backed away, hesitating to step further into the sitting room, but it was too late.

"Oh, you've got to be kidding me." Vander's rage-filled words cut through the room. "You're fucking the faerie?!" he yelled, pushing past me and the sofa to corner her where she stood. "What kind of twisted game are you playing here, fae? You may have been able to charm my brother, but I see right through you."

"Vander, please! We have more important things to worry about right now." I followed him to where he had Aerie pinned, desperate to get him and his shadows now coiling through the room away from her.

"Can't you see, brother?! She's poison for our tribe. The fae can't be trusted." He pushed me off him, never letting his gaze leave Aerie's as he wrapped a shadow around her body.

"Brother." I lowered my voice, trying not to let my anger get the better of me. He held her in his grasp, waiting to strike like a venomous snake. Aerie closed her eyes, swallowing hard as she tried to remain calm beneath his hold. Seeing her strength, despite the threat that now held her, twisted something inside me. I wouldn't let him harm her further—not after all she'd done to heal, after the pain and grief I knew still tormented her. I reached for my axe again, one hand raised to Vander in a fruitless attempt to settle him.

Vander must have heard the shift in my tone or noticed the axe once again in my grasp, because he finally turned his attention towards me. "Don't tell me you're actually defending her," he sneered.

"Vander, if you'd just back away and let her go, I'll sit down and explain everything to you."

"Fuck that," he threw back. "Don't waste your time. There's nothing you could say that would convince me this"—he gestured between me and Aerie—"is okay."

"If you'd just—"

"No!" Vander shouted, making the whole room go still. Aerie's muscles twitched and I knew she was feeling the surge of his power through her limbs. She pursed her lips together, the faintest tremors overtaking her body as she let out a slow, terrified breath. "This is what their kind does!" Vander pointed back to where Mirren's little body lay, bloody and unconscious. "So, no," he added, his voice returning to a moderate level. "Don't bother explaining anything." He started to walk away, ripples of shadow wafting in his wake, a harrowing mark of how much rage was building inside him.

"You don't have to tell me how cruel the fae can be." My heart broke as I heard Aerie's pure, soft voice speak out over the room. It stopped Vander in his tracks. He turned slowly back towards her.

"Aerie, you don't have to—"

"No." She argued to me, taking a deep breath, as if acknowledging the weight of whatever words hung on her tongue.

"My father was one of the last fae kings." She raised her chin, unwilling to back down as Vander's eyes burned into her. Pride swelled in my chest as I watched her step forward. "His plan had always been to strengthen my powers in preparation for the day he'd find the most ideal fae male for me to marry. His hope was that I'd pass along all that power to a worthy heir. I was nothing more than a conduit, a breeding ground for him to restore the fae hierarchy."

My face fell slack, the tension and anger I'd felt towards Vander suddenly gone as Aerie's words poured out. It was like a tap she couldn't turn off now that she'd finally let it flow. And there was nothing I could bring myself to do besides stand there and listen in shock.

"My ancestors told myths of an ancient fae ritual—a passing of magic. It involved a lot of traditional nonsense, rules about when and how things needed to be done. It was often used in times of war, when fae kings would overthrow each other and wanted to claim the right to their kingdom. Or in blood lines to keep power pure as new heirs replaced old ones."

Aerie fiddled with her hands, clasping the bed sheet around her as her strength faltered to give way to the unease beneath. Her eyes found mine for a moment and I offered her a small, reassuring nod. Her gaze darted over to Vander, who stood unyielding—but listening as shadows radiated around him. Her eyes didn't linger long on him before finding the ground again as she pushed on:

"My father, however, had found a way to use it to his advantage, passing along the magic from members of the tribes to me as a way to reclaim the power he insisted the Fates stole from us."

Even Vander's shadows stilled at that confession. Aerie gave it no notice.

"When I was younger, he'd capture a tribe member every few years, killing them in a ritual sacrifice and forcing me to drink their blood to take on their power." My heart dropped, a threatening growl slipping from Vander at Aerie's words. But she didn't let it deter her as she pressed on. "I didn't question it. For a long time, I just let it happen because it was a part of my life for as long as I could remember. I'd like to say I didn't know any better, but even as a child—I knew it wasn't right."

She paused, clearly struggling to admit whatever dark secrets still lingered within her. Members of my tribe who had disappeared over the years, under my watch—under my father's—flashed through my mind. I couldn't help but wonder if any of them had fallen victim to her father. If they had met their fate at the hands of a mad fae king and we had never even known. My skin prickled with anger as I added this to the list of transgressions I'd one day make her father pay for.

"But as I got older," Aerie continued, pulling my mind back to the present, "he started forcing *me* to kill the captives, claiming I could only truly inherit every ounce of their magic if I was the one performing the rituals—the one taking their lives." Her voice shook as she spoke, weighted with guilt and pain for the blood spilled by her hands.

My body went rigid, my eyes slowly swaying to where Vander stood. It was a deep confession for her to offer him, given how little he trusted her already. It was a lot to wrap my mind around, my own emotions crashing in waves of confliction against each other. But I had no doubt that Vander wasn't conflicted in the least. He would use this as evidence that Aerie couldn't be trusted. He would use this as judgment to kill her.

He cut a look to me as Aerie stifled a sob and tried to regain her composure. I shook my head at him slowly, palming the axe still in my hand. He was entitled to his opinions, but I would not let him near her. Not after everything she'd trusted me with.

"I understand if you can't accept me after hearing this." My head snapped back to her, tears glistening in her ice blue eyes.

"Aerie," I breathed, shaking my head as I stepped up to her. Not being next to her, not comforting her when I could see the pain fighting to overcome her, it was killing me. I was frozen in shock and on guard, aware that Vander posed a real threat to her here—especially after that confession. Perhaps I was even a little hesitant, trying to determine how to feel after everything she'd admitted. But I cleared my head from all that noise, my body finally snapping into action as I took in the sight of her.

I brushed her hair out of her face, wiping away the tears that had escaped and cradling her cheek in my free palm. "What he made you do was terrible. But it was all his making, Aerie. I could never blame you for the vile things you had to do at his hand." I paused, raising her gaze to meet mine. "None of this changes anything for me. All it does is make me hurt for you more. You should have never been treated in such a way, and as far as I'm concerned, that blood is on his hands, not yours. Even if you were the one holding the knife."

My fingers trailed over her hair, down her neck, and onto her bare shoulder. A sickening thought turned over in my mind and I closed my eyes, letting my forehead fall to hers as I lowered my voice. "Is that how you got the scars?"

I could feel her small nod against me, my stomach dropping in disgust and hatred as she confirmed what I feared.

"The passing ritual was just one of many ways my father tried to strengthen my magic. The scars are just proof of all the methods he tried, rituals and experiments he found over his years of research. At some point, I don't think even he knew what he was doing. He just enjoyed watching me suffer."

"Prove it." Vander's voice sliced through the room.

I growled at him, seething at his demand. She owed him *nothing*.

Vander ignored me as he stepped forward. "Prove you're a traitor to your kind. That this isn't all some kind of elaborate ruse to trick my brother into trusting you."

"Vander," I swore, cutting him a cold look at his newfound level of absurdity.

She said nothing else—didn't even argue as she turned around, faced the wall, and let the bedsheet slip off her shoulders to reveal the scars covering her back and sides.

I clenched my jaw to tamp down on the anger storming inside me as she sidestepped me to let Vander see the tapestry of terror her father had carved into her skin. I had felt each of them beneath my fingertips, silently counting them while she slept in my bed. I would make her father pay for every mark, just like I told her I would. I didn't care how long it took me to hunt him down.

I turned to watch my brother. He at least looked as shocked as I was at Aerie's confession. It had caused him to pause long enough to tame some of his shadows. Perhaps to even reconsider his bias.

"My father," Aerie called out loud enough that Vander would hear. "He gave these to me. They, among many other things, are the reason I ran away." She bowed her head, letting him look as long as necessary to understand.

His eyes traced the scars, absorbing the horror that they represented—and the truth that they confirmed. My fists clenched at my sides, furious that it had come to this, that Aerie felt the need to justify herself to him when I knew how hard it was for her to talk about that past.

"That's enough." I cut a look to Vander as I replaced the bed-sheet around her and tucked her under my arm. I could sense the shift in his magic. It still stormed around the room, but it was no longer directed at Aerie. His body was still stiff, rage-filled, but it felt like Aerie's confession might have actually convinced him of her innocence rather than confirming her guilt in his mind. "Perhaps its time, brother, for you to learn that the world is not as black and white as you believe it to be." I let my gaze bore into him, my threat filling the space between us before continuing. "And if you will be under *my* roof, then you will not threaten her again."

Vander's jaw stiffened, but he didn't argue. His gaze lingered where Aerie had been, as if still picturing the scars in his mind. I willed his attention back to the unconscious little fawn draped across the sofa, still wounded. "We can discuss this all later. Right now, Mirren needs us."

CHAPTER 16
AERIE

My chest heaved, my hands shaking as I let go of the confession. This truth had haunted me for so long, it felt bizarre to finally be free of it. Especially when I looked into the eyes of the dark creature I'd finally chosen to admit it to. It was likely a foolish decision to bare my soul to Vander. It was a risk giving him more reason to distrust me. I didn't know why I'd chosen this moment to admit everything. I just needed them—needed Bastian—to know that I wasn't the same as my father. No matter how much Vander wanted me to be.

Bastian moved roughly through the room, whether from anger or exhaustion, I wasn't sure. Vander stood back, giving Bastian room to kneel beside the small body on the sofa. I lingered on the edge, my eyes trained on Vander. Seeing the child so mangled, so broken, it had unraveled something in me. I'd lost count of how many lives I'd taken before I finally found the courage to stand up against my father. They haunted my dreams, even to this day. Sometimes it wasn't even a name or a face that haunted me, just the sheer amount of blood that had been spilled at my hands.

A chill ran down my spine as, even now, I saw their faces, felt their presence weighing on my soul. Sometimes I feared they would never leave me. That they would haunt me till the end of my days as retribution for our senseless violence. Sometimes I feared even more that they might leave, and I'd lose sight of the path that led me to who I was today. That I'd grow cold and indifferent—numb after years of shame and guilt.

I inched forward, peeking over the edge of the sofa to where the child lay. Blood covered her face, matted in her sandy brown hair. Her limbs jutted out at unnatural angles, causing my stomach to turn. I knew then that I didn't want to forget. No matter how much it hurt, I couldn't forget them, the lives I took or the ones lost because of their association with me. I squeezed my eyes shut, trying to refuse the sting of tears behind my eyes as my sisters' faces flashed across my mind. They were dead because of me, and no matter how much torment I endured by remembering, it was how I honored them. My penance for their sacrifice. My way of undoing all that my father had done.

Bastian's eyes met mine. I found sorrow and fear there, a plea for me to do something, to help her. Bastian's hands hovered over her too-still body, unsure what to do. I pushed down the fear and contempt that was threatening to overtake me after everything that had happened between us, coming around the sofa to join Bastian.

"Let me help," I offered quietly, wrapping the bedsheet around my body and tucking it securely against itself. My eyes still darted between Bastian and Vander, not fully trusting where I'd landed with the latter. My body instinctually shrank away as Vander cautiously stepped forward. Bastian threw a hand out, warning him to stay back. He huffed out something under his breath, arms straining to control his rage as he folded them across his chest.

Bastian moved, sliding himself between me and Vander. His amber eyes replaced Vander's dark and merciless ones as his face filled my vision. He nodded at me in reassurance as I took a deep breath and stretched my hands out over her. They shook with the fear that still consumed me, but I was tender in my touch—careful not to cause her any more pain than she was already in.

"Get me a bowl of water and some clean linens to clean her up. I'll start working on her wounds." My voice was weak, still struggling to return to normal after Vander's shadows had constricted against me. I tried to shake off the feeling of his shadows on my skin, but couldn't help but notice their presence still in the room. It took me a moment to reach for my magic, my mind reeling from the chaotic events of this damned night. The strength of Vander's magic still had a hold on me, still struck fear in me even as I tried to push it out and let my own power through.

Bastian mumbled something to Vander as I focused on the child before me. Vander grumbled but disappeared into the kitchen. When he returned, he had the things I'd asked for. I watched his movements out of the corner of my eye as he set everything down on the nearby end table, being sure to back away to his corner once he had. The space between us and the momentary relief from his penetrating stare had allowed my magic to find its way through my hands and out across the girl's body.

Her marred skin began to glow golden, working to heal the parts of the child's body that had been left damaged after the attack. Bastian's gaze bore into Vander as I worked, only breaking to hand me clean linens or take the soiled ones from me. I could feel the amount of pain and terror the poor girl was in, the paralyzing weight of it crushing what little life was left in her spirit. I imagined that same tranquility that I'd let envelop Bastian when he'd allowed me to take away his pain flooding the child's mind.

Despite the hate Vander had given me, despite the distrust I could still feel radiating off him at the sight of me healing this child, I would do what I knew best. He might believe me to be a vile fae, scheming and stealing and only ever looking out for myself, but I would show him all that my sisters had shown me: benefit of the doubt, acceptance, love, and light. I would show him that I was more than my fae upbringing, that I was nothing like them. And I would start with this fawn, letting my magic fill every wound and piece her back together. Not because Vander deserved it, but because she did. And maybe, somewhere within me, I could relate to the image of a broken, bleeding girl who'd been cast to the side and left to find a way to survive on her own.

The brothers sat on the sofa opposite me, discussing the details of the attack and arguing in hushed tones as I sat next to the child I now knew as Mirren, stroking her soft brown hair. I'd cleaned her up as much as I could, wrapped her in some fresh linens and discarded her soiled clothes, making sure to pour as much healing magic into her as I thought her body could stand. Healing wasn't as simple as just a snap of the fingers and things being as good as new. It was a strong form of magic, one that could easily break its recipient if not used with caution and care—as my father had so easily proven with me.

I looked down at the sweet child lying across my lap, her face so innocent and pure. Even in the midst of the horror she experienced, it didn't seem to stain her the way it would most. My heart broke for the memories I was sure would linger from whatever torment she went through tonight.

"Where is she to go, brother? Where is safe for her right now? " Bastian's words were filled with anger and guilt. "We made a promise to Lennox and Kirwan to protect her."

"And we've failed," Vander bit back, just as vexed as his brother, just as riddled with guilt. "I don't know where to go from here, but I cannot entrust her safety to anyone else. Not after this."

Bastian scoffed. "You've been gone since the day Hazlenn disappeared. What makes you think you can come back after all this time and settle into the routine of doting daddy dearest?" Vander growled in irritation. "I'm not trying to harm you, Vander. It's a serious question. Do you really think either of us are the best solution here? She deserves a stable environment to grow up in. She'd been through enough as it is."

"And what is your solution then," Vander chided. "Throw her back in another home? Trust that whatever compassionate tribe member soft enough to take her in can somehow miraculously protect her too?"

Bastian sighed, frustrated and clearly exhausted from the night's turn of events. "I don't have a solution, Vander. I'm just trying to think out decisions before they are made purely off heightened emotions."

The weight of silence settled over the sitting room. Neither brother would look to the other, instead watching the little fawn's chest rise and fall with each breath she took.

"Let me look after her." The words were out of my mouth before I'd even realized what I was saying. I was as shocked as both brothers looked.

"Absolutely not." Vander's response wasn't all that surprising, but I noticed it lacked his usual resoluteness and bitterness. Like perhaps even as he rejected the idea, he was mulling it over in his mind.

"Aerie, are you sure you're up for a responsibility like that?" Bastian's voice held nothing but concern. For me, for Mirren. It had me pausing, looking back to the child even as I continued stroking her hair. I couldn't explain it, but somehow I felt like perhaps this was where the Fates had been leading me. To her. Maybe even to him. Who was I to question their intentions?

I nodded firmly. "At least until I'm ready to leave. It will buy you both some time to find a more permanent solution. A better one."

A muscle in Vander's jaw feathered as he watched me with deadly intent. Bastian waited, letting his brother have the final say—but I couldn't help but notice the way his shoulders sank at my response.

"Fine," Vander ground out. I wasn't the solution he wanted, but there weren't a lot of options for him at this point.

"I'll keep her in my room tonight," I said, gathering her tiny body up in my hands. "We can get a better option set up for her tomorrow." I nodded my goodbye and carried her down the hall. I slowed my steps as I disappeared into the dark, trailing slowly as I walked in order to overhear the brothers.

"I don't like this, Bastian. I don't trust her."

"Give her a chance. She may just surprise you. And honestly, I don't think a better soul exists to care for Mirren. This is where she belongs."

I paused at my door, letting Bastian's words turn over and over in my mind. Was he referring to Mirren? Or me? I squeezed my eyes shut, trying to calm the avalanche of questions that accompanied that statement before I slipped into my bedroom and closed the door silently.

I laid Mirren on my bed, lighting the candle on my bedside table to illuminate her tiny features. In a matter of weeks I went from the comfort of my home with my sisters, tucked away in the woods for no one to find, to being brought into the tribe's borders, falling for the chieftain, and taking on the responsibility of caring for one of their own.

I buried my face in my hands as I sank to the floor, letting my back rest against the cool stone wall. I didn't know what I was doing anymore. My life's path had never felt more confusing or chaotic. I'd told myself this would be a temporary stop, a stepping stone onto whatever journey I would find next. But the longer I stayed here, the harder it felt to imagine ever leaving.

Letting Bastian go was one thing. It would be hard but not impossible. He didn't need someone like me in his life anyway, not when he had a tribe full of people who would rather see me dead than by his side. The more I thought about it, the more I was actually thankful for Vander's return. He was exactly the reminder I needed that this could never work.

Mirren stretched in her sleep, her mouth popping open as her arms reached out above her head before settling back in on her side. The candlelight danced around us in the emptiness of the room. It had only been a matter of hours but I was already bonding with her, growing an attachment I was fearful I'd never be able to break.

I curled up beside her, watching the steady rhythmic movement of her chest. The rise and fall of a normal breathing pattern. The sign of life that she hadn't shown when she was beaten and bloody on the couch. I hadn't told Bastian or Vander, but she'd been so much closer to death's door than I think either of them realized. Had I not been here, they wouldn't have been able to save her, wouldn't have been able to get her to a healer in time.

I knew right then and there that if anything was going to keep me here, it was her.

"Don't worry, little fawn, nothing's going to harm you anymore. I've got you."

CHAPTER 17
BASTIAN

"Are you going to tell me what happened or are you going to just sit there brooding?" I shoved a glass of sunbeam whisky into Vander's face as I took my place beside him on the sofa.

"I told you," he gritted out. "Kahlis attacked. Again. One of his creatures got in and started wreaking havoc on the nearby town."

I watched my brother cautiously, his anger from everything tonight still brimming on the surface. "And you just happened to be there when everything went down?" I replied, raising a brow.

"I was trailing Khalis when it happened, in hopes that he'd lead me to Hazlenn. Not that I have to explain myself to you." Vander sipped from his glass, refusing to make eye contact with me.

I hesitated to ask my next question. "Did you find anything? Any sign of... her?"

Vander ignored me, draining his glass and setting it down so hard I was sure the glass would break. "The town will need you to be there as soon as possible." He stalked over to the counter just off the sitting area, grabbing the bottle of spirits and discarding his glass altogether. "I'm sorry if that cuts into your faerie fucking, but you have a responsibility to this tribe first and foremost." He took a long, deep swig from the bottle, fixing me with a hate-filled stare.

I sighed, bringing my hand to my head as I rubbed at my temple. Tonight's turn of events was spurring a headache and I was too tired to argue further with Vander. About any of this.

"Brother, I did not expect you to understand what is going on between me and Aerie. Fuck, I didn't even expect you to find out. I haven't seen you in almost a year aside from the offhand moments you decide to storm about the estate and leave again without giving me even a hint at what you've been doing out there."

"You *know* what I'm doing out there," he threw back, taking a heated step towards me.

I rose to my feet. "Yes, looking for Hazlenn. But fucking Depths, brother, would it kill you to check in once in a while? Let me know that you're actually okay, or better yet, alive?"

Vander's anger seethed from him, the room filling with dark, threatening shadows. "Someone has to be out there, searching for her. What do you expect me to do?"

"And someone has to be here, running the tribe," I argued back.

We both fell silent as we recognized the burdens the other carried.

"I don't need you to like her or understand us, Vander. But I need you to get your rage under control around her, and trust that I can handle these things myself."

Vander sneered, letting out a harsh laugh. "I will never be okay with you choosing a fae to take to your bed, Bastian. No matter if she claims to be different. Not when Kahlis has torn apart our family and killed everyone we loved."

"She's not like him, Vander. She's proven that tonight. None of this is her fault." But Vander just shook his head in blind rage as he paced the sitting room. "I thought if anyone would understand the stronghold on my heart, it would be you."

"*Don't.*" Vander spun around, spitting his anger in the single word. "Don't you dare sit there and compare what I feel for Hazlenn to whatever fuckery is going on between you and that fae."

"And don't stand there and act like you're the only one who's able to do anything in the name of love!" My voice shook the walls, my feet suddenly beneath me as I rose to meet his anger—throwing it right back at him. "You aren't the first male in the world to find the one you're fated to, brother, and you certainly won't be the last." My chest heaved with the passion I put into my words, the authenticity I hoped he could sense dripping with each confession.

He threw an incredulous look my way. "*Fated*?"

I cursed my mouth for letting it slip, before I'd even told Aerie myself. That I had fallen, totally and entirely. Not even tonight's confession could change that. And I couldn't be bothered with Vander's opinion on the matter. Every day, I lost more of that ability to care if my tribe came to tear this place down and us with it. I would lay down my life for her, would spend the rest of my days fighting for her, for us.

Vander was watching me curiously, surely reading things in my silence. He grimaced, taking another heavy drag off the bottle of sunbeam whiskey still in his hand before setting it on the counter and walking towards the door. He paused there, looking back at me over his shoulder.

"Does she know? How you feel?" His question was so quiet I almost wondered if I'd heard him right.

"I—" I stammered, unsure how to answer. "We haven't discussed it yet."

He swallowed, biting back some sort of emotion that was fighting to break free. "Tell her." His voice was raw as he called out to me. "Tell her while you can."

And with that, he slipped back out into the night.

Once Vander left, I retreated to my room and got dressed in my riding leathers, strapping my battle axes to my sides. The town that had been attacked would need me there, and based on how Vander spoke of the horrors he'd witnessed, it couldn't wait till morning.

I made my way through the halls and knocked softly on Aerie's door, hoping it wouldn't wake Mirren. Aerie cracked the door open, sleepily peering into the darkness of the hallway.

"How's she doing?" I asked, nodding towards Mirren bundled up on Aerie's bed.

"She's doing great, all things considered. I've been continuing some healing sessions throughout the night, but for the most part she's just been sleeping."

I nodded, letting Aerie's words calm some of the worry still racing through my blood.

"She's a bit of a cuddler," Aerie added, stifling a smile as she looked up at me through those long, beautiful lashes. I laughed quietly along with her.

"Good, good. That must be a sign of something positive, right?"

Aerie noticed my clothes, the twinkle in her eye instantly falling away to make room for concern.

"Are you leaving?" She sounded scared. Not that I could blame her.

"Yes, I have to go check on the town that was attacked. See what there is to be done, what little bit I can even do for them at this point. It sounds like it was a massacre. I'm going to have a sentry stationed outside of the estate while I'm gone. The town is close. I should reach there before dawn. But just in case you need anything, he's out there."

"Okay." Her voice was small and I wanted more than anything for her to say more. It wasn't okay. I hated leaving her safety in the hands of someone else, hated leaving her without discussing the weight of everything she'd admitted tonight. I knew she hated it too.

"He doesn't know who you are, I just told him you're recovering and he's been ordered to leave you alone. He won't be close enough to see you. Just look after Mirren and I promise I'll be back as soon as I can."

I leaned in to kiss her forehead, the motion causing her to take a step back. Her eyes were soft and apologetic, but there was a hardness there too. Like she was forcing distance between us. I hated leaving things like this, us on two separate pages about where we were, what we wanted. I closed my eyes to take a calming breath before taking her hand and planting a kiss there instead. I turned away, every step in the opposite direction painstaking. It felt like ripping my very heart in half and leaving a piece of it here. So much was undecided, so many things left unsaid. But I would do this for my tribe, for the lives lost tonight at the hands of the monster that continued to tear apart my life. And then I'd find my way back to Aerie and Mirren. I'd tell her how much I loved her and how I needed to have her in my life. Not just for now but forever. Because, no matter how hard I tried, I couldn't imagine a life without her by my side.

CHAPTER 18
AERIE

I spent the entire next day worrying about Bastian—what he would see, if he would return safely, how he must have felt about everything I'd confessed. Mirren was an easy distraction. She needed much attention after last night, her mental and physical health both severely strained even with my magic. But no matter how much I let her occupy my time, I found my mind repeatedly returning to my night with Bastian and what it meant for us moving forward.

I didn't know how to admit to myself what I wanted from him. What I wanted for us.

Mirren, despite all she'd been through, was settling in nicely. She was responding well to the additional healing sessions and was coming alive with each passing hour within the estate. It was hard not to feel joyous in her presence. She took to me immediately and we spent the day exploring the estate rooms together. I hadn't had the opportunity to venture out much since arriving here, and seeing everything for the first time through her eyes was exactly what I needed to distract me. I hadn't been able to pull much out of her—the trauma from the attack most likely affecting her ability or desire to speak—but her eyes shone brightly as we wandered from room to room. We danced around the library, twirled through the halls, and settled in for a warm dinner of nourishing vegetable soup. By the time the sun set, I was tucking Mirren in for the night and sitting with her as she drifted off to sleep.

I carefully slipped off the bed and tiptoed across the room once I was sure she was sleeping deeply enough to not rouse at my absence. I left the door cracked enough so that I'd hear if she woke while I tidied up for the night.

I returned to the kitchen, intent on cleaning the rest of the dishes from dinner and possibly baking something for breakfast in the morning. I lit the hearth in the corner, letting the firelight illuminate the otherwise empty room. I noticed something on the other side of the kitchen out of the corner of my eye, jumping as I turned to see what was there.

"Fucking Fates, Bastian." I clutched at my abdomen, forcing air into my lungs to calm the terror pumping through my veins. "You frightened me. I never heard you return." I moved towards him, noticing as I spoke how still he was. How sunken and sullen he appeared as he sat in his chair in the corner of the kitchen. The bottle of whatever spirit he'd offered me on my first day here sat beside him on the kitchen table.

"Bastian." His name rang through the kitchen like a desperate prayer. He finally looked to me once I got close enough. Tears streamed down his face, mixing with the blood and filth that coated his skin.

"There was so much blood, Aerie. So much death." His voice shook when he spoke.

I stepped closer, his knees parting to let me close the distance between us. I cupped his face in my hands, smoothing my fingers over the stains and grime covering his cheeks, wiping it all away along with the tears he cried. His hands trembled as they slid up my legs, hooking around and holding onto me so tightly. I brought his head to my chest, embracing him and holding him—holding the weight of his grief for the members of his tribe that he had lost.

"Let me take away the pain, Bastian." I couldn't imagine the responsibility he felt as chieftain of his tribe, the burden of leading so many lives besides his own. And I knew him well enough to understand that this was the result of him taking on the blood spilled this week, the lives lost. There was nothing he could have done, yet he felt the guilt of their misery. He mourned the loss as if they were his own blood. It was an honorable thing to do as a leader, but it was a heavy burden to bear.

Bastian's breath heaved, but he nodded against my chest—finally agreeing to let me help him. I backed away, clasping onto his hand and guiding him up. Slowly, I led him through the estate and to his bathing room. Turning on the tap to fill the tub, I sat him down by the hearth and told him I'd return in a moment. I made my way across the hall, tiptoeing into my room and grabbing a few ingredients out of the supplies Bastian had purchased for me. I checked on Mirren before heading back to Bastian, ensuring she was fast asleep and safe still.

Bastian hadn't moved at all from where I'd left him. He was staring at the floor wringing his hands as he waited for me to return. I led him back into the bathing room, turning off the tap and filling the water with the herbs I'd brought back with me.

"Take off your clothes," I instructed as I leaned over the tub. I plunged my hand beneath the surface, letting the warmth of my magic heat the water as I swirled in the floating bits of petals and leaves. A golden hue rippled around my fingers, mixing with the churning water. Bastian was beside me then, naked and dazed and still tear-stained as he took my hand and let me help him into the tub.

I bathed him in the silent darkness. No words passed between us but with each scrub of his skin, each wave of water rinsing his body, I let my warmth wash over him. Slowly but surely, life revived within him. His shoulders slumped less, his tears stopped, the weight lifting ever so slightly. I helped him back out of the tub when I was sure I'd cleaned every last speck of blood and dirt from his body, grabbing a nearby towel and drying him off.

"Better?" I asked as I stood back to assess him.

He didn't answer, didn't move. He just stared at me, a certain kind of intent in his eyes that I couldn't quite comprehend. Within an instant, he closed the distance between us, wrapping his thick hand around the nape of my neck and kissing me hard. It was so different than our first night together. Then, he'd been slow and careful—now, he was hungry and desperate. His tongue didn't wait for permission before it claimed me. I scrambled to return his passion, his desire, as I pushed back with my own lips. My own tongue claimed his mouth as I pawed at his arms, his back, anything my hands could find purchase in.

He didn't break the kiss, didn't allow for space between us even as he grabbed the length of my dress. The fabric grazed my sensitive skin as he brought it up my body, the pace a taunting speed. His lips were gone in an instant, a flash of cotton material overwhelming my sight before he found me again, discarding my dress in a pile at our feet.

He ran his hands down my back, over my ass, and gripped hard at my thighs before lifting me from there. I was in the air clinging to his neck as he carried me out of the bathing room and to his bed just a few steps away. He set me down gingerly, laying me on my back and hooking his hands under my knees to pull me to the edge of the bed.

"Do you trust me, Aerie?" The question surprised me, especially in the passion of this moment. He'd been so desperate to have me in the bathing room—did he really want to talk about this now? I pushed up on my elbows to look at him, still crouched on the floor in front of me.

"Bastian, why are you—"

He cut me off, holding up a hand. "I asked, do you trust me?"

I swallowed hard, all the thoughts and hopes I had for us circling through my mind. I didn't know how we'd ever make those a reality, but I couldn't bring myself to lie to him in this moment.

Not after he'd allowed himself to be so vulnerable with me, let me see that burdened side of him.

"Yes," I nodded slowly. "I trust you."

A smirk fell over his face, that same one that always got under my skin.

"Good," he answered. "Then lie back and close your eyes."

I did as he said, even though I didn't quite understand what he was doing. I took a deep breath, preparing myself for whatever he was planning. But as he picked up one of my ankles and started planting kisses up my leg, desire bloomed at my core. He let my knee fall to the side as he continued his path up my inner thigh, stopping just shy of my center, before setting my leg back down and starting the same path on the other.

By the time he got past my other knee, I was grinding against the sheets, desperate to feel him consume me.

"Bastian," I begged.

He hummed in approval as he made his way up my other thigh, stopping annoyingly short of exactly where I wanted him. He set my foot back down, making sure to part my knees wide enough to give him room.

"Still have those eyes closed, Aerie?" I squeezed them tighter in response, nodding desperately in hopes that he could see the motion. He hooked a thumb around my undergarments, tugging them softly down my legs.

"Good girl." The way his voice purred as he talked to me pushed my need for him further. My hips scrunched down the bed in a desperate attempt to have him on me. His mouth, his fingers. I didn't care how he took me, I just knew I wanted nothing in this world more than for him to claim me wholly and fully.

I jumped in surprise as I finally felt his tongue graze my center. Not being able to see his motions or know what was coming had me on edge, but it heightened my other senses in ways I hadn't expected. It intensified the feeling of his mouth on me, licking and sucking as I climbed higher and higher.

"Please, Bastian," I cried out again.

"That's right, Aerie, keep saying my name." His words vibrated against me, pushing me further—right on the edge of freefall.

"I need you," I panted. "In me." My breath was ragged, my lungs begging for more than I seemed able to get down. Bastian answered in a punishing groan against me that had me grinding against his face in return. With a final flick of his tongue he was up and hovering over me. His face glistened with my desire and I bit down on my lip as I watched him lick his own.

He leaned into me, pressing his length against my middle as he kissed me hard.

"You taste like fucking sunshine, Aerie. I could spend all my days between your legs and never go hungry." He rested his forehead against mine as he spoke, and I let an unruly smile break across my face at his words.

Before I could respond, he was standing over me again, running his hands down my sides. He grabbed my hips, his fingers digging into the soft flesh as he turned me over in one swift move and raised my ass in the air. I suppressed the urge to squeal at the sudden movement, painstakingly aware of how on display I was for him in this position.

He stepped up to me, running a single finger from the base of my neck down my spine, my ass, and finally over my center, plunging deep within me. I gasped, the sound stuck somewhere between a cry and a groan as I leaned back into him.

He pumped his hand a few times before sliding back out and finding that sensitive spot, caressing it in steady circles as he lined himself up with me. He sank into me, taking his time over and over again. It was torture, paired with the way his fingers stroked and swirled against me.

"More," I choked out as he backed off for what felt like the millionth time. I heard his laughter, deep and gravelly as he teased me again.

"I'm teaching you the art of patience, Aerie," he chided as he pulled me onto him, sinking himself fully within me. I cried out in need, hoping he'd understand just how much I wanted him to keep going.

"Plus, I promised you I'd be gentle, remember?" he said as he removed himself completely. This was a new kind of torture. I felt empty, incomplete without him inside me and I whimpered at the sudden lack of him.

"Forget being gentle." My voice was breathy and rough with need. "Fuck me, Bastian."

His grasp on my hips tightened in desire, taking just a moment to line himself up once more.

"You don't have to ask me twice, Sunshine." He slammed into me, hitting just the right spot as he gave me a moment to adjust to the feel of him. He picked up his pace, giving me exactly what I'd asked for. Something that had been woven tight within me finally snapped as I came utterly undone to his steady rhythm. A few more thrusts and he was chasing my release with his own, falling over me and catching his weight with his arm.

He rolled beside me on the bed, pulling me into him to rest my head on his chest. Spent, exhausted, and out of breath, we soaked up the otherwise silent ambiance of the room as he stroked steady circles along the bare skin of my back. Each movement outlined the scars there, causing me to curl into him further, feeling nothing but safety and acceptance here by his side.

CHAPTER 19
AERIE

We lay in the silence for what felt like forever. I didn't ask about what he saw at the town that was attacked, I knew he didn't want to talk about it here. I just wanted to enjoy this moment with him. Here and now. Because in this moment, I was his. I didn't have to worry about my future or the heartbreaking reality that I'd never be able to call this place my home. I didn't have to think about the grief and guilt weighing heavy on my heart or the loss that I'd endured. With him, so much of that floated to the background. It was still there, the pain was still real, but he just made it all so bearable.

"Aerie." The way he said my name felt like a form of worship.

"Hmm?" I was too ensconced in the bliss of this moment to form any actual words.

"Marry me."

I sat up, pushing off his chest with a hand as I whipped my head back towards him. "What?" I blurted out.

"I love you, Aerie." He reached out, running a hand through my unruly hair. "I want you to marry me, to start a life together here, to spend every day just like this."

I gaped at him, unsure how to respond to such an abrupt confession.

"I—" I stumbled over my words, my mouth moving faster than my mind could keep up with. "I don't know what to say to that."

"Yes is always an acceptable response." His lips tipped up at the corner, watching the shock and confusion battle over my features.

"Bastian, I can't marry you," I replied in an exasperated voice. I climbed out of the bed, searching for the sleeping gown he'd pulled off me in the bathing room.

"Why do you say that?" He pushed himself up on the bed into a sitting position. I scoffed at him, as if there weren't a million obvious answers to that question.

"Well for starters, I'm fae."

"And?" His tone was annoyingly at ease, like we were talking about something as simple as the weather or what to eat for dinner.

"*And*, you're a chieftain for one of the tribes. In no world would our union ever be accepted by your tribe." I was pacing the room now, unsure when I'd gotten dressed or started walking. He watched me intently from his spot on the bed, but he kept his tone level and casual as he spoke.

"They'll accept whoever I trust enough to weave my life's thread with."

I fixed him with a hard stare, letting him know just how ridiculously improbable that sounded.

"Don't worry about them, Aerie. We'll figure out how to navigate those moments when we get to them. What matters is what you want, not what they think."

I shook my head, returning to my pacing as I tried to allow my mind a moment to catch up with everything he was saying.

"What is it that you want, Aerie?"

I didn't answer, couldn't answer as I wore a path into the floorboards with my incessant steps.

"Aerie."

I couldn't open my mouth, couldn't form a response worthy of voicing.

"Aermidh." He stepped into my path, forcing me to stop. I hadn't even noticed him get off the bed. I looked up at him through wide eyes. Eyes that I was sure were full of terror.

"You don't want me, Bastian." My words were barely a whisper between us. Had he been any further away he wouldn't have heard them. He smiled at me, but there was pain in his eyes as he held my face in his hands and wiped away a stray tear that had fallen down my cheek.

"Yes, I do, Aerie. I want you every day from now until eternity. I can't imagine a life without you."

I shook my head, refusing to believe that this could be real. It was more than I deserved.

"You're just caught up in the moment. You don't truly want this."

Bastian's jaw flexed in frustration. "No, Aerie, I've been thinking about this for much longer than I should have." He sighed, resting his forehead against mine." Do you remember the slabs of wood I laid out next to the garden?"

I nodded, unsure how that had anything to do with this. That day in the garden felt like an eternity ago. So much had happened between now and then.

"It's for you, Aerie. A wedding gift. I was marking measurements to build you a greenhouse for all of your herbs and plants. A place where you could practice your craft."

"A greenhouse? For me?" I blinked back more tears, begging them not to fall as I looked to Bastian in utter confusion. How could he have known back then that he would ask me this?

"For you," he affirmed. "Because from the moment you walked into my life I knew I couldn't let you go. This—what we have—it's too important to let you walk away."

I turned away, my chest aching with the effort it took not to give in to him, not to run into his arms and let him take all my pain away.

"I don't care how much you try and deny it. I know you feel it too. The fates have brought you into my life for a reason, brought us together for a reason. Don't turn away now that it's getting real."

I folded my arms over my chest, feeling suddenly too exposed in front of him. "Bastian, I've done things. Things I'm not proud of. I bear too many scars, carry too many burdens to ever be with someone like you."

He came up behind me, wrapping his arms around me and fully enveloping me in his embrace. I leaned my head back against his chest, hearing the steady rhythm of his heart.

"Give me your burdens, Aerie. Let me help you carry them. I'll bear your scars every day. They weigh nothing to me, not when it means I get to have you. Let me be your strength so you don't have to carry it alone."

I couldn't hold the tears back, finally letting them spill over my lashes as I scrambled desperately for anything to push this male away. I didn't deserve the love he was offering.

"You're chieftain, Bastian. And I'm a ruined fae who is unable to produce an heir. Your tribe will never stand for that."

Bastian spun me around to face him. "Fuck what they want, Aerie! They are nothing to me if they mean I can't have you."

"You don't mean that," I whispered.

"I do! I will walk away from all of them. The tribe, Vander, anyone who tries to tell me I can't have you. *You* are my home, Aerie. *You* are my family. Fuck the rest of them. If they mean I can't have you, then fuck them." His hands trembled with a silent sort of rage as he looked down on me. He looked so powerful, so strong as he fought for us—and I'd run out of points to argue.

"I've spent my life in hiding, Bastian. First with my father and then with the coven. I don't know how to do anything else."

He took my hands in his as he spread our fingers out together, entwining them as he once again closed the distance between us.

"We'll figure it out. One day at a time. And if it's truly not what you want then we'll run away. You, me, Mirren—we'll pack up and run away together. I don't care where we are, what we're doing. So long as you are with me."

I let my eyes find his, searching for anything deceitful or hesitant. I was met with only the purest, strongest of intent. I had fought for so long to find safety, fought the nightmares that haunted me, and fought to hide who I truly was. Perhaps it was time to stop fighting. Perhaps it was time to find a place to land, a hand to hold, and a partner to help carry the weight. As I did for him tonight, as I'd do time and again if given the opportunity.

"There is no part of you I couldn't love," he confessed, his voice like gravel. "No piece of you that would scare me or cause me to turn away. You just have to let me. Please, let me."

I failed to hold back the sobs as they overtook me, my body and my mind breaking down at the thought of someone being able to love me so fully. But even as my mind tried to reject it, something deeper within me knew it felt right. He was right when he said this was his home—it was mine too. The way it felt like agony when he wasn't by my side, how my mind settled and the grief lifted when I was with him. There was so much I still didn't believe, so much I didn't know how we'd handle it. But if he was this confident that we could figure it out together, then maybe I could be too.

I wrapped my arms around his neck, stretching up to reach his lips and kissing him in a slow, gentle way. When I pulled back, I rested my face against his.

"I love you too, Bastian." The words felt as easy as breathing as they left my lips. I thought I'd regret saying them, thought they'd bring only more heartache and confusion. But as I felt his smile against my cheek, as the true implication of everything those words meant settled around us, I realized this was exactly where I was supposed to be. No matter how crazy it was, no matter if this wasn't supposed to happen between us, I knew without a doubt in my mind that this was exactly where I wanted to be.

He was right when he said the Fates had brought us together. And if he'd fight as hard as he had tonight for us, then I'd fight too.

Bastian held me as we leaned against the headboard, my head resting against him. My fingers traced circles over his chest, my mind lost in thought of the absolute whirlwind that these last couple months had been. Everything had happened so fast. The loss of my sisters. Bastian finding me and bringing me here. Us falling for one another and finally accepting that fate. Mirren coming to us and all the responsibility that came with raising not only a little one but one who'd been through the horrors she had. It was so much so fast. And I couldn't help but worry that perhaps it was all a little too fast.

"What's on your mind, sunshine?" Bastian's voice was a low rumble. I could feel the vibrations in his chest as I leaned against him.

I thought for a moment, trying to make sense of exactly what question was circulating in my mind. "Are you sure this is what you want, Bastian? Given everything that's happened... everything that you now know—about me?" I closed my eyes, waiting for him to respond.

His silence filled the air for a long moment. Too long, I realized. Perhaps he really wasn't sure and had just been waiting for me to give him an out. I peeked up at him, terrified I'd find a look of contemplation or relief on his face.

Instead, he was staring down at me, shaking his head.

"You're right," he answered at last. My stomach dropped as I sat up. "I don't want this, Aerie. I *need* this. I need you. What else do I have to do to convince you this is it?" A surge of relief flooded my veins, making my heart beat heavily. "You are my future, my love. No matter your past. No matter what you've shared with me or whatever darkness you may still have tucked away within you."

He leaned forward, wrapping his hand around the nape of my neck and pulling me in for a gentle kiss. "I will spend every day of the rest of my life trying to convince you how deserving of love you are." His words danced across my lips, caressing my skin as I leaned into his touch.

My eyes shone with new tears watching him sit back and take the deepest, darkest parts of me in stride. He'd created the space for me to let that burden go, even though I could tell it pained him on some level to hear what my father had done to his people. Never once did he direct that pain towards me. In my mind this had felt like such a heavy secret, something that would keep me from ever moving forward with my life. But in this moment I realized, letting go of that secret—freeing that guilt by sharing it with him—it might in fact be the one thing that would allow me to finally escape my father's grasp. I smiled to myself, suddenly feeling freer than I had in decades—and I relished in that feeling.

"So," I said, settling back against his chest as he returned to his spot leaning against the headboard. "What does a wedding to the big bad chieftain look like? I assume it entails a lot of traditions and planning." I sat up quickly, turning to meet his gaze as a thought occurred to me. "We don't have to participate in some sort of tribal sex ceremony, do we?"

Bastian barked out a laugh, letting his head tip back towards the ceiling. I lay back down, content with his reaction to my question and assuming I didn't have to wrap my mind around any weird tribal traditions.

"No," he finally answered once he got his laughter under control. "Nothing like that. I was actually thinking of something much more simple."

"Hmm?" I hummed against his chest, feeling the weight of sleep pulling me down.

"Maybe something like you and me in the woods, weaving our life threads together under the light of the full moon."

I smiled against his chest. It sounded perfect, something I would have picked myself—which I knew was exactly why he'd suggested it. The full moon was what led him to me, how we first laid together, and it only seemed fitting that it was how we promised forever to each other, too.

I breathed in his intoxicating, smoky scent and prayed a silent prayer to the Fates, thanking them for weaving our life threads together, for bringing me the one person who could perhaps help me finally be free of my father and the spirits haunting me. There was a time in my life that I wasn't sure what my purpose was. My sisters offered me a home, a place to heal, and I would be forever grateful for their help during such a haunting time in my life. And I would never get over that loss.

But being here with Bastian, wrapped in the safety of his arms, it felt as easy as breathing. As easy as existing. There were still so many challenges left for us to overcome, so many unknowns and obstacles. But in this moment, they simply melted away, leaving us with the purest kind of magic. This love was a force to be reckoned with, a kind of magic I'd never experienced before. It felt like finding myself, like even if I tried to walk away right now because of all the reasons I'd tried to deny him, I wouldn't be able to. We were two forces, caught in each other's pull—living and breathing with one heart, one soul.

I let that singular thought radiate around our entwined bodies, tucked into each other so tightly I was sure there was no room left where our skin didn't touch. He needed me and I needed him, and there would be no denying the weight we would carry for each other. Two halves of the same whole. Two hearts beating as one. Two life threads that should never have crossed, yet here we were—so woven together that it was impossible to tell where one ended and the other began.

EPILOGUE
BASTIAN

I stood beneath the hemlocks, my head tilted up towards the sky as I watched the clouds part and give way to the fullness of the moon. I basked in the light it offered, soaking in every detail of this moment, this night. A priestess from the moon tribe waited beside me, dressed in her formal robes as Mirren lingered quietly beside us. Aerie had insisted on giving her a basket of petals for the ceremony, and I found myself smiling as I watched the sweet girl run her fingers through the plant matter. She released petals one by one to fall to the forest floor, letting the night's breeze carry them off and watching to see how far they'd travel before releasing the next one.

The priestess seemed to enjoy Mirren's task as much as I did, leaning over and whispering something in the girl's ear that made her lips tip up as she handed the priestess a few petals from the basket. I was lucky to catch her before her return to Sgàil's borders. The moon tribe served as our recordkeepers, among many other things. And unions—especially ones amongst the leaders—wouldn't be respected unless recorded and overseen by one of the priestesses. She had been the only soul I'd told about our plans, the only one who would join us on this sacred night. That is, unless my brother decided to show.

I let out a deep breath, releasing with it any hopes of seeing him here tonight. Shortly after Aerie accepted my proposal, I'd snuck out into the Dark Woods. I'd done it countless times before, whispering secret prayers into the shadows of the trees in hopes they would somehow get back to my brother, wherever he might be. It was the only way I could think to contact him, the only hope I had that perhaps one of these days he'd hear me and return home for good. As much as I understood his need to search for Hazlenn, I couldn't help but admit I was beyond lost here on my own.

It was never my job to be chieftain, never my responsibility to care for the estate and the tribe, leading all on my own. Even when he'd taken the title of chieftain after our parents had passed, he'd had my help. We worked together on these matters and made a vow to always be there for the other, because we were all the other had left. This past year had been more than taxing without him, without anyone here to help me navigate this new territory I'd found myself in.

I pushed back the thoughts, clearing my throat as I let the raw emotions of the past fall to the wayside. It wasn't time to dwell on such things. I didn't want this day marred with the dark stain of grief and loss that seemed to follow my family throughout the years. I rolled my shoulders, willing the nerves ravaging my body to fall away with the motion.

A noise within the trees pulled my attention as I settled a hand against the battle axe strapped to my side. It might be a sacred night, but I refused to come out here without some sort of protection, especially with both Mirren and Aerie here too. A shadow slipped through the forest, causing my hackles to raise as I freed the axe from its harness and slid myself between the form up ahead, and Mirren and the priestess waiting beside me.

"Is that any way to greet your brother?" The familiar voice snaked its way through the trees, settling my awareness while simultaneously shocking me to my core.

"Vander?" I called out as he stepped from the shadows.

"You sound shocked, Bastian. But it was you who asked me to be here tonight. Did you really think I wouldn't come?"

I didn't know how to answer, because I honestly hadn't expected him to show.

"You heard my message?" I asked tentatively. Vander motioned over to the shadows still trailing in his wake.

"The shadows are always whispering to me, telling me things they've seen." He looked back to me, fixing me with a look that sent ice down my spine. "Things they've heard. It was foolish of you to declare your plans to the Dark Woods, Bastian. I had to come, just to be sure you weren't getting yourself into even more trouble." He moved closer to me. I was even stunned to see that he'd actually dressed for the occasion. I didn't know where or how he'd acquired the formal clothing, but I found myself suddenly pushing back tears as he took my hand and let his other arm wrap around my shoulders in a firm, rigid embrace.

"Brother, I may not agree with your particular choice of wife, but I will be here for you if this is what you choose."

"It is," I choked out, trying not to lose all semblance of control as my brother held me in his embrace. It felt like a past life, an easier time when we weren't tainted with the harsh realities of the world we lived in now. Too much loss, too much blood had pushed us apart. But he was here now, making good on his vow as my older brother, and I couldn't help but hope that despite his shadows, there was still some of that goodness left within him.

He released his grip, backing away and crossing his arms over his chest as he took in the sight of me. "She makes you happy?" he asked, finally.

"More than I can even try to explain," I answered.

He gave me a firm nod, but it was impossible to miss the hint of a smile playing at his lips. Without another word he dropped to his knee and began speaking softly to Mirren, playing with her as she twirled around the trees and scattered the petals from her basket. The sight warmed my heart, seeing us piece together some semblance of a family from the wreckage of our lives. I opened my mouth to say as such to Vander, hoping it would bring him as much joy as it brought me, but caught movement from the trees out of the corner of my eye.

My breath caught in my throat as I looked to Aerie stepping through the trees with divine grace as she made her way into the clearing. The fabric of her somehow familiar gown glowed as it caught the moonlight, the material draping around her like it was made for her and her alone. I felt the need to clutch my chest, seeing her here like this. It was overwhelming, almost too much to take, too good to be true. She was a vision, a phantom, a siren's song that couldn't possibly be here, walking towards me. But she was, and she had a gleam in her eye that had me crumbling beneath her gaze. Vander raised to his feet and backed up beside me as she made her way over to us and reached out a hand for me.

I clasped onto it like it was my very own life's thread, wrapping my arms around her and breathing in that familiar scent I'd come to crave with every fiber of my being. I pulled back only far enough to find her lips with my own, chasing down the glorious taste of her as she parted for me, begging my tongue to take more. This was what our forever looked like, that savage need to always have more of each other. It was a desperate hunger that I hoped I would never satisfy.

Vander cleared his throat behind us, causing Aerie to pull back, and I gritted my teeth in annoyance at his interruption. But as Aerie backed away, forcing space between us that I was sure neither of us wanted, I found my voice once more to ask what I was sure was on both mine and my brother's minds.

"Where did you find that?" I asked, gesturing to the beautiful cascade of satin material hugging every curve of her body. She smoothed her hands over the front, and my hands flexed in desire as I watched her fingers trail over her hips.

"I went through some of the old trunks and wardrobes around the estate in search of something for tonight." She paused, noticing the way both me and my brother had fallen silent. The way neither of us could take our eyes off her.

"Is that okay?" she added tentatively. I couldn't answer, just stared in adoration at the sight of her in that dress underneath the moonlight.

"It was our mother's." Vander cut in for me. His voice was raw with emotion, just as I knew mine would have been if I'd found the courage to speak. Our mother's. Aerie looked like one of the goddesses reincarnated as she stood amid the forest in my mother's dress, capturing every ounce of her beauty and grace. I didn't know how she'd found it, but I couldn't help but take it as a sign from the Fates, the earth, my mother herself that this was supposed to happen.

"Are we ready?" The priestess ushered us to join her.

"Absolutely," I answered as I grasped Aerie's hand once more and brought her to stand beside me. I didn't make out one word of the priestess's prayers and vows as she quoted from our tribal traditions, asking us to swear ourselves to each other. I couldn't think, couldn't process anything other than Aerie standing before me. I let my eyes slide over her body, pressing every detail into my memory—praying I'd never forget this.

Aerie reached over, unclasping the battle axes from my sides and laying them between our feet. I looked between her and the priestess, brows furrowed as I tried to understand what she was doing.

"A fae tradition," she answered, as she let that warm glow of her magic flow from her fingers and down into the blades settled on the grass beneath us. "A piece of me to carry with you into battle. To protect you when you need more strength. And a guide to bring you back home when you lose your way. May your aim always be true and your steps always lead you home."

The golden light faded away, leaving in its place an intricate etching against the metal. I stared down at the blades, then back up to her as my heart grew full to bursting with the love and appreciation I carried for the female standing before me. I bit back the tears threatening to expose my emotions.

"Aerie, I will spend every day of the rest of my life finding my way home. Back to you. No matter the distance, no matter the difficulties we face. It will always be you and me."

She lowered her head, smiling as I spoke. But I could feel the doubt she still held, even now. I caught her chin with two of my fingers, lifting her gaze back to me. "I'm deathly serious, Sunshine. I will never stop loving you, never stop pursuing you. There is no force within this world or the ones beyond that could keep me from you. From my home. And I need you to know that, I need you to accept that here and now."

The smile fell from her lips as she searched me for any hint of deceit, any ounce of doubt or indecision. When she found none, she nodded her head.

"I need to hear you say it, Sunshine. Out loud."

"Yes, Bastian, I accept it," she answered. "And I, you. Don't for a second think that only goes one way, chieftain."

A smile grew on my weary lips, accepting at last that she truly believed me, truly received my promises to her. This was the start of forever. Her and me against all odds, overcoming all obstacles. A little runaway fae and the big bad chieftain, as she loved to call me. We might carry burdens unimaginable for most. And we might have a hundred more things to work out together. But that's how we would do it. Together. Because she was my mate and I was hers. Together we would figure out what our future held. A life together, leading a tribe neither of us were supposed to, raising a child that didn't belong to either of us. It was a messy, grief-ridden future, but it was ours nonetheless.

As I took her face between my hands and brought her lips to mine beneath the light of the full moon, I vowed to her, to the Earth, to the shadows of the Dark Woods, to the Fates themselves and anyone else who would listen, that I would spend every day of the rest of my life fighting to protect what was mine.

Acknowledgements

This little novella was an absolute joy to write, so I'm going to try and keep the acknowledgements in the same manner—short and sweet. I've had Aerie and Bastian's story in my mind since I started writing my debut novel, A Tether Through The Rift. I wasn't sure how I would incorporate their story into this series, but thanks to my amazing readers who pushed me to write this novella, the world gets to experience their love like I always hoped they would.

I couldn't write this acknowledgement section without mentioning my wonderful husband, to whom this book is dedicated. He is my rock, my best friend, and if it weren't for him I wouldn't know how to write this kind of love story. He has helped me heal, helped me grow, and continues to push me to challenge myself every day. He is my true life partner and I can't imagine a day where I won't start my acknowledgements by thanking him for all of his support and encouragement.

I also have an incredible team of alpha and beta readers. This is my second time going through this process, and so many of my readers have stuck around and even filled bigger roles for this novella. I'm blown away by their endless support. Every late night chat, endless streams of voice messages, and all the brain storming sessions... I wouldn't have been able to do any of this without them. Thank you for putting up with my insanity and showing me what true friendship looks like.

To Myanna, my artist and right hand man. Girl, your artwork is published! You are officially a cover artist, through and through. Thank you for taking a chance on me and stepping outside your comfort zone. I am so luck to have you by my side. You have been such a huge support to me, in every way. Not only have I found my go to artist for all of my writing, I've also found one of my closest friends.

To my editing team, Sophie and Julia. Thank you so much for helping me make this novella shine. Y'all are both truly bright, gifted, and diligent souls, and you have no idea how grateful I am for your dedicated work with my writing. You both have been with me now for two books, and I can't imagine a better duo to get my work ready for the world. Thank you for caring about these projects as much as I do.

And lastly, to the author community that I've found myself in. Thank you so much for creating a support system that I can rely on. Y'all are always there to lend a hand or give moral support when I get into a rough head space or feel overwhelmed. The indie author life is a hard one, but y'all make it just a little less confusing and scary. I feel so lucky to have found friends like y'all and I hope one day I can return some of the same support that y'all have given me.

If you're looking for some other indie authors to support, check out any of these amazingly talented names: K.M. Davidson, C.A.

Blooming, Monica Amore, Rebecca Quinn, Alexis L. Menard, and Elle Mitchell.

ABOUT THE AUTHOR

Lindsey N. Rhoden is a mom to four crazy kiddos, full-time homeschooler, devoted wife, and a (sometimes more than) part-time writer. Located in the North Texas region, she has spent the last few years as a birth and postpartum doula and photographer, specializing in the art of Ayurvedic and herbal care. She enjoys nature, herbalism, and obviously lots and lots of reading. You can often find her cuddled up at home with a fantasy book, a cup of matcha, and one of her big dogs or her cat by her side. And probably one of her four kids crawling on her.

Her journey through motherhood and her struggle with anxiety and depression helped rekindle her love for the written word after a long reprieve through college and early adulthood. After a particularly rough season in 2022, she decided to dive back into writing—and found out that she apparently has a lot to say.

To stay up to date on upcoming work from Lindsey N. Rhoden, be sure to follow her on social media @booktrovertbynature or check out her website at www.lindseynrhoden.com

IF YOU ENJOYED A LOVE WOVEN IN MOONLIGHT,

Be sure to check out the first book in this series, A Tether Through The Rift!

MAGIC MAY BE A GIFT, BUT IT WILL ALWAYS LEAVE A MARK.

A Tether Through The Rift is a wonderland-esque, dark fantasy romance about the journey of learning to love and accept oneself. Join Hazel in this harrowing story full of nature-based magic, dark villains, and well hidden secrets lurking in the shadows.

READ ON FOR AN EXCLUSIVE EXERT!

CHAPTER 1
HAZEL

*T*he wind was a bitter rush against my face, jolting me awake and pulling me back into the clutches of pain and terror vibrating through my body. I was flying. Long, leathery appendages dug into my body; claws ripped into my skin. I didn't need to open my eyes to know where I was, or at least to know what was happening to me.

It was a dream. That dream.

Slowly I forced my eyes open and peered down to the land looming below. I would have been more scared if it wasn't for that sight. I let loose a shaky breath, taking in every inch of that beautiful world flying past—like somehow I knew it was the last time I would see it. Breathtaking wasn't even good enough to describe it. Yet my breath hitched. It did every time I dreamt of it. My eyes pored over every extraordinary detail, desperate to hold on to any part of it, to find a way down into it. It was unlike anything I had ever seen in real *life. I couldn't think of a single thing to compare it to. But here in my dreams, it lived.*

Forests made of the deepest green I'd ever seen, endless seas of velvet grass flowing with the occasional wave of wildflowers, small cottages and vast estates made of stone and wood, so like the forests and meadows surrounding them. It was impossible to tell where nature ended and civilization began. Instead, it just merged together in a beautiful, fantastical cascade. I wanted to live here, to know here. But I couldn't stop flying. It was not my own strength that propelled me forward, but rather some dark force that held me, moved me against my will. I wanted to linger in the beautiful peace of that world below.

I didn't want to press on. I knew what came next.

And as quickly as it appeared, that world of deep greens and warm sunlight disappeared and I was plunged into darkness. It surrounded me—consumed me—as I plummeted down. My arms flailed for anything to grab onto, trying to save myself. I found nothing, just as I did every time this dream reared its ugly head. Next would come the screaming, like that of some dark creature desperately hungry and out for blood. Out for my blood. Even though I could barely see my hands through the darkness, I knew they were covered in the sticky, red liquid. I could smell the metallic tinge of its scent heavy in the air—could feel it dripping, heavy and slow down my arms. Whether it belonged to me or to someone—something else—I did not know.

I hit the ground with a sickening crunch that promised no less than one broken bone, trying desperately to get my feet underneath me and start running—running and tripping and falling over myself in a chaotic attempt to escape those screams. I knew my life depended on it. I didn't dare stop, despite the fact that my legs felt heavy as stone. A wave of terror hit me as I wondered if I was even moving at all. It seemed entirely possible that I was merely treading water, so to speak. My eyes squinted, trying to adjust to the emptiness around me. It was useless. There was no adjusting to pure darkness. That's what I had fallen into. Pure, relentless black. I kept running though, hands thrown out in front of me to keep from crashing. The screams were getting closer. The vibrations of its powerful stride rattled my bones as it tore through the space separating us. Those long, piercing claws I'd felt around me earlier were now nipping at my heels, my back. There was nothing I could do to get away, no hero coming to save me. I could feel my body relenting to the exhaustion pulling it under, could feel it slowing down and willing my mind to give up. Just as those cruel, taunting claws dug into my skin, I awoke.

I lay there for a few minutes, waiting for my mind to return to my body. It was like I was drifting between two worlds: not wholly in this one yet, still retreating from another. My mind was lost to whatever lived there. I'd had this dream for as long as I could remember. Which, if I was being honest, wasn't long. I couldn't remember anything prior to one year ago, when Arlo had found me out in the woods on his journey between towns. Anything prior to that was a complete mystery to me. When I felt my awareness return and was confident that I could stand up without fainting or puking, I swung my legs off the side of the bed and sat up, pressing my clammy palms into the hollows of my eyes. My head was pounding from the fear rushing through me.

I reminded myself I was safe. I was here. Just like Arlo taught me. I looked over to where he was lying in the bed, fast asleep and looking more perfect than ever. The lines of his face were more relaxed than when he was awake, his concern for me taking a momentary reprieve while he slept. I didn't know what I'd do without him. I wouldn't have survived long in this world if it weren't for him. I debated waking him, telling him I had the dream again, but I thought twice and decided to go wash up instead. He had enough to deal with; he didn't need me running to him every time I had this nightmare.

I tiptoed over to the bathing room and eased the door closed, trying to soften the click of the latch. A bath was often my remedy for a night full of bad dreams and restless sleep, the comfort of water causing both my body and my mind to feel weightless. I turned the faucet handle all the way on and sat with my head in my hands while I waited for the tub to fill with the tepid water. Thoughts of pain and blood flooded my mind as soon as I closed my eyes. I fought back the tears as I took three deep breaths.

How could that pain feel so real? It was just a dream.

I blinked back the tears threatening to spill as I peeled off my sweat-soaked clothes and climbed in. The endless list of questions circled in my mind as the water coiled around my body. *Why does this nightmare haunt me? What does it mean? Who was I before I showed up here? Why do I feel like I don't belong, can't belong here?* I could feel the water reaching up to pull me under, and I welcomed it gladly. Despite the sweat that still clung to my skin, I found myself longing for warmth, wishing I had taken the extra time to heat a kettle and pour in the boiling water before I'd climbed in.

I sat there like that for a long time, long enough to let the feel of the water drown out the endless thoughts. When I felt like my mind had settled somewhat, I pulled the stopper for the drain and stepped out of the comfort of the bath and into the chilled air of the bathroom, wrapping a towel around my body to trap as much warmth as I could against my skin. I stared at myself in the stand up mirror situated in the corner of the room, the reflection disrupted somewhat by the speckled fogginess of the glass. My green eyes stared back at the pathetic image in unkind judgment. My auburn hair hung around me in wet, dripping clumps, circling my shoulders and falling down my back in deep red contrast to my skin which looked too light – too tired. The dark circles under my eyes reminded me of how little sleep I was getting these days. I breathed out a disheartened sigh, letting my gaze fall away from the mirror and down to the floor. I heard a soft knock and looked up to find Arlo leaning against the doorframe. His beautiful, slender form was backlit by the sunlight pouring in from our bedroom.

I found myself incapable of focusing on anything other than the way he stood there, looking at me.

"Was it the dream again?" Arlo asked, concern etched on his face.

I nodded. I might be broken and dysfunctional, but with him standing there, the morning sunlight glowing around him like some sort of god, I didn't care about any of it. He was my silver lining, my light in the storm. He had an uncanny ability to pull me back from the edge of my darkness. And I hoped one day I could return the favor, although I doubted he would ever need it.

He pushed off the frame and took a few steps into the bathing room, wrapping a hand around the back of my head and kissing my brow.

"It's okay, Hazel. I've got you." He paused before adding, "You know it's not real, right?"

I nodded again. Although I didn't know how convinced I was that he was right, or how convincing I was to him with that nod.

"I know, it just *feels* so real. I don't know how to shake it when I wake up."

"This right here? This is real," he said. He hooked a finger under my chin, lifting it toward him, and kissed me. Soft at first, as if to make sure I'd allow it. Then deeper to remind me how real this was.

I smiled against his lips and kissed him back.

"Always the chivalrous knight," I said. "What would I do without you?"

"Be hopelessly bored, I'm sure. And not nearly as satisfied." He pulled back with a wink and placed his hands on my shoulders. "You are okay, though?"

His concern was more than genuine; I could see it on every inch of his sun-kissed face. It had been bad before... This wasn't like then. In my worst moments I'd struggled to understand what was real and what was just part of my dreams. I'd kicked and screamed at invisible threats and cowered in the darkness of our bedroom for fear of anything lying in wait beyond. He couldn't tell when I was okay or when I was getting bad again because the battle was in my mind. I constantly had to remind myself that he couldn't feel those emotions or hear those thoughts. That was my curse, not his.

"I'm fine, 1 promise. Just a rough night."

He eyed me for a minute, trying to decide whether to accept what I said or push me a little further.

"Good," he finally said, with one more kiss on my forehead. "I'll go make us some tea."

He turned to leave and I watched as his elegant form disappeared around the corner, into the kitchen. I inhaled a deep breath and sighed a little as I let it out. He was another question I hadn't figured out.

What had I ever done to deserve a man like him?

Something told me I'd never get the answer.

I emerged from the bedroom, dressed in my favorite cozy wool tunic and a pair of leggings. Arlo was measuring out tea leaves as I strode over to the bread and jam waiting on the middle counter and tossed a couple pieces of the loaf on to the stove eye to toast.

I took a minute to just watch him. His golden brown hair fell slightly on his forehead as he bent over our mugs, his amber eyes focused on the water he was pouring into them.

The memory of the day he found me slowly crept back into my mind. He'd had that same concentrated look in his eyes as he sized me up and tried to figure out what exactly he believed about me. He had found me, out of my mind and wandering in the middle of nowhere. I'd told him that I had no idea where I was, no idea *who* I was. I was trembling, covered in dirt and blood. I remembered that gleam in his eye, the recognition of utter terror, and what I felt was a wave of empathy washing over him. I was hysterical—completely inconsolable. Yet he helped me, believed me.

It was complete luck that he had found me at all; we were so far from any of the local towns. He walked me to the nearest village and got me seen by the healers. He insisted I get checked out to make sure I was okay. He stayed by my side the entire time, even as the Guard was brought in to question me, and even when I realized I had nowhere to go once the healers cleared me to leave. I never understood how someone could do that for a stranger. I asked him about that at one point, and he told me he just knew. He took one look at me and knew that he was meant to protect me, love me. That he had been put on my path that day, not by some coincidence but by some higher power that knew I needed him. I thought it sounded crazy at first, but he continued to prove how true that was on a daily basis.

I had needed him then, and I needed him now. The nightmares that haunted me constantly were like shredded remnants of that day refusing to let me move on.

He turned, two steaming mugs of tea in his hands, and cocked his head to the side.

"What?" he asked.

I shook the reverie from my mind and realized I was standing there like a fool with a jar of jam in one hand and a butter dish in the other, totally lost in the memory of that day.

"Nothing," I lied. "You just never cease to amaze me."

"Because I made us tea?" he asked with a little chuckle. "I mean, I know I make a good brew, but I promise my magical abilities stop there."

He glided over to our kitchen table and set down our mugs. I jumped a little as the smell of burning bread wafted through the kitchen, remembering what I was supposed to be doing. Grabbing the bread off the cast iron stove, I threw it down on our plates and juggled everything over to the table to sit down across from him.

"So, any plans today?" he asked.

I handed him a plate and started coating my toast in the creamy butter.

"Not much. I was thinking I may head down to the library, do some more digging."

I had become obsessed with digging for answers about my past, searching the town's records and archives for anything that was remotely similar to my situation. I devoured it with a desperate sort of hunger. If and when I couldn't find any more content to look over, or the weight of it all became too heavy, I'd wander the library's other sections and look for a good book to get lost in. Yet another one of my coping mechanisms, it would seem. I firmly believed there was nothing a bath, a good book, or a soothing cup of tea couldn't solve—aside from my memory loss, obviously.

Arlo paused mid-sip and gave me a quick, concerned glance. I knew what he was thinking. That I shouldn't spend so much time cooped up in the library. But I honestly didn't know what else to do with my time. Feeling at home in this town was hard enough, let alone trying to find a purpose along with it. I knew no one—had no family, no friends. All I had was my crusade to find answers about my past.

"Hazel, maybe it would be beneficial for you to find something better to fill your time with. Something healthier, I mean. I know you want answers, but there's only so much good poring over those archives is going to do."

I knew he was right, but I couldn't help rolling my eyes at yet another argument about it. He thought half the information I came home with was complete nonsense—just lore the locals came up with because they were bored and looking for extraordinary meaning in the ordinary, everyday events of our world. I wasn't sure if the stuff I had found was true or not, but I figured I'd take a look at anything that might give me even a clue about my past or what had happened to me.

"If it will make you happy, I'll limit my time there today. And I'll make sure to take a walk through the town on my way home." I knew this wasn't an argument he was going to win. He was always concerned about me digging, but he knew how much I needed answers. And he'd never stop me from doing something if my mind was set to it. He loved me too much to stand in the way like that.

"Alright, you drive a hard bargain," he said and gave me a little smirk. He took one last sip from his mug and stood up. "I need to get going. Be careful, and just come home if it gets to be too much out there."

He planted a kiss on the top of my head and walked out the front door.

I smiled, looking where he'd just been moments ago. Then, as my eyes trailed around the house, the silence crept in. I was alone. As the weight of that loneliness hung in the air, the smile faded from my lips.